One thing was no____ ____ ____ ____ ____ ____
must get away as _____ as possible.

Swinging on his heel, Viridian saw Silvane. The hardcase
was slowly heaving himself onto his hands and knees,
clearly unable to escape in his present physical condition.
Realizing that, Viridian did not like the idea of letting him
fall into the hands of the law. The marshal would not be
content with only two of the men concerned in the death of
his deputy, but was going to want to know the identity of
the third.

Having no faith in Silvane's loyalty, Viridian extended
his right arm, pointing the Remington downward. Even as
Silvane opened his mouth, meaning to plead for his life,
the revolver's hammer fell and a .36 conical-shaped lead
ball twirled from the barrel into his head.

Viridian's Trail

J. T. EDSON

A DELL BOOK

Published by
Dell Publishing
a division of
Bantam Doubleday Dell Publishing Group, Inc.
666 Fifth Avenue
New York, New York 10103

ISBN: 0-440-21039-9

Printed in the United States of America

Published simultaneously in Canada

October 1992

10 9 8 7 6 5 4 3 2 1

RAD

*For Dustine Edward Eusden,
who is as yet too young
to read my books.*

AUTHOR'S NOTE

At the request of the J. T. Edson Appreciation Society and Fan Club, I am putting the histories of Dusty Fog, Mark Counter, and the Ysabel Kid in the form of appendices to the book. This will allow the old hands to avoid repetition, but enable new readers to learn details of the floating outfit's qualifications and careers.

1

THIS COULD RUIN US!

"NEW AND MORE LUCRATIVE MARKETS FOR CATTLE!"

The headline of the *Fort Worth Herald* was in big, bold black letters which testified to the importance placed upon the story by the editor.

Raising his eyes from the newspaper, Austin Viridian shoved back his white "planter's" hat to show the receding line of his close-cropped brown hair. Then he swept his gaze around the other occupants of the Pilar Hide & Tallow Company's office.

Tall, broad-shouldered, and in his late thirties, Viridian could hardly be considered handsome. He had coarse, irregular features that were reddened and puffy from much good living. Their surly lines gave more than a hint of an ill-tempered nature. Although he still retained a good physical development, there was a bulging to his waistline that grew more pronounced with the passing of each month. Well-dressed—in a black broadcloth coat, brocade-fronted vest, white shirt with a black cravat knotted in the manner of a bow tie, yellowish-brown Nankeen trousers, Hersome gaiter boots, and a black leather gun belt with an ivory-handled Remington New Model Police revolver in

the cross-draw holster on its left side—he looked like a
hard, tough, ruthless self-made man.

Viridian was all of that. While his wife's money had
bought him a partnership in the Pilar Hide & Tallow Company, it had been his specialized knowledge that had made
the factory one of the most efficient of its kind in Texas. He
had designed the huge building, to which the office was an
annex, with all its fixtures and fittings to facilitate the rapid
killing of large numbers of cattle and the disposal of the
unwanted portions of the carcasses.

Being one of the partners, Viridian had no real reason to
work as a slaughter-man in the factory. The prices paid by
the Company for the cattle were so low that their profit
margin precluded the need for him to participate in such
an activity. He did so when the mood took him because he
enjoyed performing the task and derived considerable
pleasure from watching a large and powerful creature tum-
bling dead as a result of his expert wielding of the poleax.
It was his frequently-made boast that he could down a
longhorn—be it a calf, young steer, grown cow, or prime
bull, the factory made no distinction—more neatly and
with less fuss than any man on the Company's payroll.

Slowly Viridian looked around the table, studying the
woman and four men who were sharing it with him. The
table, half a dozen chairs, a rolltop desk, and a small safe
were the office's sole furnishings as it was used only for the
general administration of the factory. All business transac-
tions were carried out in the back room of Bernard
Schweitzer's general store in the town of Pilar. Normally
such a meeting would have been held there, or at one of
the partners' homes, but Viridian had been working at the
factory. The others had considered that the story in the
newspaper, which had been brought from Fort Worth by
Viridian's wife and Guiseppe Profaci, was of such importance that they had come to the office rather than delay by
sending word for him to join them.

Marlene Viridian was a tall, beautiful brunet with a statuesque build that her gray traveling costume—somewhat disheveled as a result of the speed with which she had returned from Fort Worth—emphasized in a most satisfactory manner. There was a haughty, imperious look about her that suggested she could be strong-willed and arrogant. She had long since lost any romantic notions that she might have harbored toward her husband, replacing them with the feeling that she had married beneath herself. Anyway, in the first place their marriage had been contracted for business reasons rather than out of love and she still controlled most of the family's money. She was one of the owners and as such insisted on being present at all of the partners' meetings.

To Marlene's right sat the senior partner. Although the richest of the four, Schweitzer invariably dressed in a shabby old suit of sober black and only rarely wore a collar and tie. He was in his late fifties, plump, practically bald, and wore steel-rimmed spectacles which made him look far more benevolent than was his nature. He was a shrewd businessman, with many useful contacts who helped the Company sell its hides and tallow.[1]

Next to Schweitzer, Guiseppe Profaci slumped in his chair. Despite his well-cut, if travel-stained, brown suit, he could not be mistaken for other than what he was. Broad-shouldered, of medium height, he looked Italian. Good living had laid a layer of fat on his bulky frame, but under it were hard muscles. A skilled builder, he had erected the factory and the Colonial-style mansions in which the partners lived.

Studying Profaci, Viridian wondered if he suspected what had been going on in his absence. He had a voluptuous, passionate wife, Gianna, who was about half his age. While he and Marlene had been on the business trip to Fort Worth, Viridian had spent much time—including two

---

1. Tallow: the harder, coarser fats of the animal's body; used, among other things, for making candles.

whole nights—in Gianna's company. There was no suggestion on Profaci's face that he knew of the betrayal, only
worry as he scowled at the newspaper.

Dressed in the kind of clothing that had been popular
among rich French-Creoles in New Orleans before the War
Between the States—gray top hat, matching frock coat,
frilly bosomed white silk shirt, flowing cravat with a dia-
mond stickpin, fancy vest, tight-legged white trousers, and
black gaiter boots—Pierre de Froissart was also about medium height; well-built, gray-haired but still handsome and
distinguished-looking. Although he displayed no sign of
being armed, Viridian knew that the black walking-cane
leaning against his chair concealed the blade of a service-
able sword. There was also a pearl-handled Remington
Double Derringer in each enlarged pocket of his vest. He
was skilled in the use of the weapons.

From the Creole, Viridian lifted his gaze to the remaining man. While grudgingly conceding that Harlow Dolman
had proved very useful to the Company on several occasions, Viridian resented his presence. He was not a partner
and the burly man objected to him learning too much
about their affairs. There were personal reasons for the
antipathy. When speaking to Viridian, Dolman always
adopted a tone which implied that he was addressing a
social inferior. Also, he was always overattentive to Marlene. Viridian was wondering what had brought Dolman
from Fort Worth. Obviously, from his appearance, he had
traveled down in the company of Marlene and Profaci. The
burly man could not think what his reason had been, the
Italian's presence had ruled out the obvious one.

Matching Viridian's height, Dolman was more slender
and very handsome. Nothing in his appearance, as he
lounged with an elbow resting insolently on the back of
Marlene's chair, hinted that he was a member of the State
Police; an organization brought into being by the Davis
Reconstruction Administration to replace the disbanded
Texas Rangers. He wore a black U.S. Army officer's Burn-

side campaign hat, with its brim down and bearing no insignia. The waist-long brown leather jacket, dark gray shirt, the dark blue bandanna knotted around his throat, skin-tight gray riding breeches, and brown Hessian boots were of civilian cut and manufacture. They set off his athletic figure to its best advantage, augmenting his curly black hair and good-looking features.

About Dolman's waist the Western-style gun belt carried a rosewood handled Colt 1861 Navy Belt Pistol—a revolver despite its name—in a split-fronted, spring-retention holster known as a "clamshell." The drop of the holster was connected to the belt by a metal swivel stud and the tip hung free instead of being tied to his right thigh. All of the Colt's trigger guard was exposed, by having the leather of the holster's front section cut down below its level.

That had been done for a purpose. When Dolman's right hand closed around the rosewood butt, its forefinger passed through the trigger guard and stabbed a flat switch on the inside of the rig. That caused the outer portion to hinge back and liberated the revolver.

Although Viridian did not accept the captain's claim to have invented the "clamshell" holster, he acknowledged— if only to himself—that Dolman was reasonably competent in its use. However, the burly man considered that he was just as good—maybe even better—with his more conventional gun-rig. The time might come, Viridian realized, when he would need to put his theory to the test. Almost everything about Dolman set his teeth on edge.

Dolman looked like a wealthy, smart, even dandified young man. There was, however, a suggestion of hardness and an undercurrent of real cruelty on his face, causing him to exude an aura of reckless disdain that attracted some women and antagonized many men.

Viridian was one of the men who found Dolman an anathema and he suspected that his wife was more than platonically attracted by the captain. That increased his feeling of hatred. While there was no love lost between

him and Marlene, and he would be pleased to get rid of
her, he intended that it would be he who selected the manner of the separation.

Taking his thoughts from Dolman and his wife, Viridian
waited for somebody to comment upon the item in the
newspaper.

The story commenced by mentioning that a herd of cattle had been driven by Colonel Charles Goodnight from
Young County, Texas, to Fort Sumner in New Mexico.[2]
While there had been other trail drives, two details set
Goodnight's effort apart. First: The three thousand head, a
much larger number than anybody had previously attempted to move as a single herd, were handled by less
than twenty men. Second: They had been sold to the Army
as food for the Apaches on the reservations, for—and this
was the point which the hide and tallow men found most
disturbing—eight cents a pound on the hoof.

"Eight cents a pound, *on the hoof!"* Schweitzer breathed,
knowing that the expression meant as the animals stood
and not after they had been butchered and dressed out. He
did some rapid mental arithmetic. "Given an average
weight of only eight hundred pounds each, that's *sixty-four*
dollars a head."

"And we're only paying *four* dollars a head, tops, with
calves thrown in free," de Froissart went on, with the accent of a well-bred Southern gentleman. "I don't like the
sound of it. What rancher's going to accept our prices
when they can get that kind of money from the Army?"

"So how long will the Army keep paying those prices?"
Viridian sniffed. He disliked the elegant Creole almost as
much as he disliked Dolman and for the same general reasons. He was also pleased to display his knowledge of business matters. "They'll not need too many cattle to feed the
Apaches and, anyway, it'll only be the ranchers in the west-

2. The full story of this trail drive is told in: *Goodnight's Dream* and *From
Hide and Horn.*

ern countries who'll take them. The rest will have to keep coming to the hide and tallow factories. There's nowhere else for them to go."

"You should have finished reading the story," Marlene suggested with asperity. "I wouldn't have come rushing back from Fort Worth if that's all there was to it."

"Listen to this," de Froissart declared, having already drawn that conclusion and continued reading. " 'While the Army's needs are limited, the trail drive to Fort Sumner has proven that it is possible to take herds of at least three thousand head for long distances and with much smaller crews than was previously believed necessary. Colonel Goodnight claims that the lesser number of men not only reduces the expense involved in making the drive, but allows the herd to be handled with greater ease and efficiency.' "

"So they'll be able to bring us bigger herds and save money on the crews' wages," Viridian grunted. "I don't see—"

"You will," Dolman promised, eyeing the burly man in a mocking manner.

" 'For some time now,' " de Froissart went on, " 'Colonel Goodnight and other ranchers have been concerned over the serious depletion in breeding stock caused by the low prices paid at the hide and tallow factories. So they have been looking into the possibility of other, more lucrative markets. Having heard that beef is in short supply and commanding high prices in the East, Colonel Goodnight has contacted buyers in Chicago and New York. The replies have been most encouraging and it is his intention to make his next drive to the railroad in Kansas. Once there, the cattle will be purchased and shipped east on the trains.' "

"I see what you mean, Marlene," Schweitzer stated solemnly. "This could ruin us!"

"Huh!" Viridian snorted, being unwilling to concede that his wife might have acted correctly in bringing the matter to their attention. "Who else will be fool enough to try taking herds all the way to Kansas?"

"Pierre still hasn't finished the story," Dolman pointed out, watching the red flush of anger creep into the woman's cheeks and being delighted by the venomous glare which she directed at her husband.

An ambitious man, Dolman had no intention of remaining a peace officer; even a comparatively important one. Especially as he suspected that the days of Davis's much-hated, generally corrupt and inefficient State Police were numbered. To his way of thinking, there was no real, or—more important—profitable future in that organization. Nor would he be acceptable in whatever force replaced it. So, what he wanted—and was determined to attain—was control of a thriving, lucrative business. The Pilar Hide & Tallow Company had struck him as being ideal for his needs. From what Marlene had told him, while making love, she would not be averse to him joining her in a bid to take over the Company.

" 'Colonel Goodnight will be attending the Ranch Owners' Convention to be held at the conclusion of the Tarrant County Fair at Fort Worth,' " de Froissart continued. " 'In addition to explaining his method of handling a large trail herd, he will be discussing the new markets for the cattle. He also hopes to be able to introduce some of the Eastern buyers to confirm his statements. Colonel Goodnight says that, if his plans are successful, the sale of cattle in Kansas will help set Texas back on her feet.' "

"He's right about that," Dolman commented, taking a malicious satisfaction from watching the anxiety shown by Schweitzer and de Froissart, the partners most capable of appreciating the danger to their Company. "The men who make the drives and sell the herds in Kansas will bring back more money than they could make by selling to you. Perhaps not as high as sixty-four dollars a head, but more than the four dollars you've been paying. And it will only be steers they'll need to take, not breeding stock."

From the expressions on their faces, not only Schweitzer and de Froissart, but Viridian and Profaci were growing increasingly aware of the facts stated by the captain.

Left impoverished and disenfranchised as a result of supporting the Confederate States during the War, the people of Texas—with a few exceptions—were in dire straits. They had no industries or mineral resources capable of bringing in revenue and their sole assets were the herds of cattle which roamed and bred prolifically across the vast miles of open range.[3]

While the cattle existed in enormous numbers, the only market for them in any quantity had been at the hide and tallow factories. As the supply far exceeded the demand, particularly since the end of the War, the price paid for the cattle was very low. So low, in fact, that ranchers were compelled to sell cows and bulls which would otherwise have been used for breeding purposes.

With only the hides and the tallow having any commercial value, the whole operation of the various factories was very wasteful. After the two saleable portions of the carcasses had been removed, the remains—including all of the meat—were thrown into the Brazos River—along which many of the factories were situated—or disposed of in a similar fashion.

"If this story's got around—" Schweitzer began, looking at each of his partners in turn.

"It has," Dolman warned. "Ranchers from all over Texas have been telegraphing to friends, or the Fort Worth hotels, asking for accommodation. While the County Fair's offering horseraces, steer-roping, and cutting horse contests, they're not coming just for that."

"How long have *you* known about *this?*" Viridian demanded, tapping the newspaper with his left forefinger and glaring at the peace officer.

---

3. It would be many years before oil became a factor in the economy of Texas.

"I've been hearing talk about it for the past two weeks at least," the captain confessed.

"And you didn't take the trouble to let *us* know about it?" Viridian challenged, pleased at finding an opportunity to put Dolman in bad with his partners.

"I thought that it was only idle gossip," Dolman countered, conscious of the accusing and reproachful looks being directed at him. Even Marlene was showing displeasure. Then he saw a way in which he might be able to turn the tables on Viridian. Staring pointedly at the burly man, he said, "Surely some of the ranchers who came *here* mentioned it to *you?*"

"Not to *me,* they didn't!" Viridian exclaimed, seeing the trap and taking steps to avoid falling into it. "How about you, Bernie?"

"Never a word," Schweitzer replied, being equally determined to exculpate himself. "But it's been well over a month since the last rancher was here. Then it was only Paul Dover and he might not have known anything about it."

"You mean you haven't had any cattle for over a month?" Dolman asked, having seen a number of animals in the factory's holding corrals.

"Only the herd that Ribagorza brought in last week," Schweitzer answered, without meeting the peace officer's eyes.

"Well," Dolman conceded, "it's not likely that *he'd* know about it."

None of the partners offered to comment on the remark, but they knew what the captain was implying. Although Juan Ribagorza had frequently delivered herds to the factory, he did not own a ranch. He and his band of Mexican hardcases stole the cattle, which were sold to the Company for an even lower price than would have been paid to the legitimate owners.

"Perhaps the ranchers are holding back their deliveries

until they've heard what Goodnight has to say," Dolman continued, after almost a minute of silence.

"They could be at that," de Froissart said worriedly. "And if his idea is accepted, nobody will bring us their cattle."

"Not even Ribagorza," Dolman supplemented. "Even if he finds it easy to—buy—the cattle he can make more money taking them to Kansas."

Once again the four owners did not feel the words called for a reply. They had always kept up the pretense of believing that Ribagorza came by the cattle honestly.

"Of course, you'll have one consolation," Dolman went on. "If Goodnight's idea works, selling the cattle in Kansas could help set Texas back on her feet."

Obviously, from their expressions, the prospect of Texas's economic recovery meant little to the partners. In fact, Dolman knew that none of them had any loyalty to the Lone Star State. Only de Froissart was a native-born Southerner, but the place of his birth had been New Orleans. Of the others, Schweitzer and Profaci hailed from New York and the Viridians had originated from Boston. As Marlene's accent showed, she had been born and raised in the wealthy, socially elite Back Bay district. Her husband, however, had clearly sprung from much humbler surroundings.

"To hell with Texas," Viridian blazed, expressing his companions' and wife's sentiments. "It's *us* that I'm concerned about."

"What can *you* do about it?" Dolman challenged in a mocking manner.

Catching the implication in the captain's voice, Viridian pushed back his chair and came to his feet. Standing and glaring about him, he resembled a longhorn bull that had scented danger and was preparing to defend itself.

"Get to Fort Worth before that son-of-a-bitching Convention starts," the burly man answered. "And make sure

that nobody believes there's a market for their cattle anywhere except with the hide and tallow factories."

"That's the idea, Austin!" Schweitzer praised. "Will you
need any help?"

"I can't do it alone," Viridian replied. "So I'll take Gus
Roxterby along. He can do the hiring while I keep in the
background."

"Smart thinking," de Froissart exclaimed. "That way nobody will know that we're involved."

All the partners approved of Viridian's selection.
Roxterby, a tall, lean, sharp-featured man whose range
clothes usually bore traces of dried blood, was the factory's
floor supervisor. However, they suspected that before joining the Company he had made his living at least on the
fringes of law breaking. Certainly whenever the necessity
had arisen, he had always known where to locate the kind
of assistance that was required.

"When're you leaving, Austin?" Profaci wanted to know.

"As soon as we've got one thing settled," the burly man
answered.

Viridian was no fool. Realizing that what he had in mind
would involve breaking the law, he meant to take precautions. One of them would have to be against betrayal or
desertion by his wife and partners if he should be arrested
while carrying out his illegal work.

2
A SHORT-GROWED,
BLOND-HAIRED KID

"Well I'll be damned!" the lean, gray-haired rancher said, with relief, peering at the centerman of the trio who were confronting him. He allowed his right hand to drop away from where it had been hovering above the butt of his holstered revolver. "It's you, Mr. Viridian. I didn't recognize you first off."

There was a good reason for the speaker's wary attitude and comment. Instead of being dressed in the fashion which he usually adopted around the factory, Austin Viridian wore—with the exception of his boots—the attire of a cowhand. He had neither washed nor shaved since leaving Pilar, traveling by a roundabout route so that he avoided the stagecoach trail and the chance of meeting people who might identify him. So he looked unkempt and far different from the way in which Paul Dover had become accustomed to seeing him.

Nor were Viridian's companions likely to produce a feeling of security or peace of mind when being met in an otherwise deserted alley on the fringes of Fort Worth.

At the best of times, Ed Silvane and Stan Timson would never pass as honest, church-going citizens. Hard-faced, dirty, cold-eyed, and unshaven, they looked what they were: a pair of hardcases, ready, willing, and able to use the guns which were hanging at their sides. Silvane was tall and lanky, Timson being shorter and thickset. Flanking their employer, they stood slightly to his rear.

The other owners of the Pilar Hide & Tallow Company had not accepted Viridian's decision to visit Fort Worth without discussion. While agreeing that something must be done to protect their interests and to counter the threat to their profits, there had been some debate as to how this might be brought about.

The first stumbling block had come with Captain Harlow Dolman's warning that he could not help the partners in his official capacity. Being aware of most Texans' mistrust of and antipathy toward the State Police, Governor Davis had ordered that none of its members should be in Fort Worth during the period of the County Fair. There would be a number of ranchers present, men of considerable influence and growing political importance, whom it might be unwise to antagonize. So the Governor had stated that the enforcement of law and order must be left in the hands of Marshal Rupert Grillman, an honest and respected son of the Lone Star State, and his deputies. That meant the Pilar Hide & Tallow Company would not have the tacit approval of the local peace officers for their actions.

In the end, it had been decided that Pierre de Froissart would attend the Ranch Owners' Convention as the Company's official representative. He was to convey the impression that he and his partners approved of the attempts to find new and more lucrative markets for the cattle, even if doing so might reduce their own profits. By doing so, it was hoped that he would be able to divert suspicion from the Company if the Convention should be disrupted.

De Froissart was well-suited to his task. Unlike his partners, he had the background and upbringing which made him socially acceptable in the best circles. So he had always acted as the link with such influential people whose support, approval, or assistance had become necessary. That had been an asset before the War Between The States and equally so once hostilities had commenced. Although ostensibly loyal to the South, the partners had ensured that more than half of their factory's products found its way into Union hands and was paid for in gold. As a major in the Quartermaster Corps of the Confederate States' Army, de Froissart had been able to organize the delivery of the goods and to prevent that side of the Company's activities from being detected. His military service now gave him an added means of access to various important Texans who had worn the South's cadet-gray uniforms during the conflict and would render him acceptable at the Convention.

While de Froissart was carrying out his assignment, Viridian—accompanied by men who had been of use on previous occasions—was to try to discredit the rumors of the new markets. He was also to attempt to persuade ranchers to sign contracts under which they would be compelled to continue making regular deliveries of cattle to the factory. Obtaining the first signatures, Viridian realized, would be the hardest part of the assignment. Once he could show that some ranchers apparently had no faith in the stories, others would be more willing to follow their lead. Everything depended upon Viridian selecting the right kind of men as his first victims. Especially as with Dolman absent the Company could not depend on the local law being sympathetic and understanding.

Luck appeared to be favoring the Pilar Hide & Tallow Company. Viridian had not been in Fort Worth for an hour and he could have hardly found a better man for his purpose. Running a small ranch, small by Texas standards, Paul Dover was not a person of any great consequence. Nor was he connected by birth or marriage to any of the State's powerful and influential families. A mild-mannered man, he had contrived to remain neutral during the War. So he could not claim the ties of friendship which military service offered. On top of that, he was devoted to his wife and children.

"I thought you hadn't," Viridian answered. "You acted kind of edgy."

"No offense meant," Dover said hurriedly. "Only there's a lot of rough fellers around Fort Worth for the County Fair."

"I know what you mean," Viridian said amiably. "It pays a man to be careful these days. Hey though, I haven't seen you at the factory for near on two months."

"Well, no, you haven't," Dover admitted, without meeting the burly man's eyes. "I've been kept busy around the spread."

"Sure, there's always something needs doing," Viridian commiserated. "Are you here for the Convention?"

"More for the County Fair," Dover answered, guessing that the main topic of the Convention would not meet with the hide and tallow men's approval. "I may drop by and hear what's being said. There's no harm in listening."

"No harm at all," Viridian agreed, sounding jovial. "Will you be bringing some cattle after you get back home?"

Suddenly, the rancher began to remember that the part of Fort Worth in which he was standing must be practically deserted. Almost everybody would be at the town's main square to see and hear Governor Davis declare the County Fair open. Having arrived later than he had anticipated, he had left his family to watch the ceremony and had brought their wagon to Mulcachy's livery barn. A chance meeting while he was unhitching the team had further delayed him, but he had felt it was time well spent.

Looking at the three men who were blocking his way to the street, Dover was not so sure that it had been.

For all Viridian's apparently friendly attitude, the rancher felt uneasy. There did not seem to be any reason for the burly man to be wearing the Stetson, wolfskin jacket, bandanna, shirt, and jeans of a working cowhand. Or to be so dirty and unshaven after the comparatively short journey along the stagecoach trail from Pilar. His two companions were hard looking and not the kind to be employed for any legitimate work around the hide and tallow factory. In addition to studying Dover in a mocking manner, they continually darted glances at the rear of the alley or over their shoulders toward the street. It was almost as if they wanted to make sure that they were not being observed.

"Well—" Dover began hesitantly, after a brief pause in which he had considered his position and drawn some disturbing conclusions. "I—er—I don't have any gathered right now and I couldn't say when I'll be getting round to doing it."

"Like you said, you've been kept busy," Viridian remarked, in a matter-of-fact tone. "There's been some talk about driving herds to Kansas and selling them for big money. What do you make of it?"

"I'm not sure what to make of it," Dover replied, trying to sound disinterested and still avoiding the other man's gaze.

"Sounds tempting, though," Viridian suggested, retaining his amicable posture.

"It sounds that way," agreed the rancher, but tried to appear noncommittal.

"It'd take too much money to set up, though," Viridian hinted.

"Not if three or four of us small ranchers get toget—" Dover began. Then, realizing that he might be saying too much, he let the words fade out. Taking the watch from his vest pocket, he looked at it. "Hey! Is that the time? I'll have to be going, Mr. Viridian. The wife's waiting for me."

"Sure," the burly man replied, watching Dover return the watch. "I know what wives are like if you keep them waiting." He grinned and extended his right hand. "I'll be seeing you around."

Watching their employer, Timson and Silvane were puzzled by his attitude. They knew why he had brought them to Fort Worth and were expecting him to take a more aggressive line with the rancher.

Relief flooded over Dover at Viridian's reaction. He had been worried about how the hide and tallow man would respond to the suggestion that he was considering the new, more lucrative, market for his cattle. Apparently, Dover thought as he accepted the offered hand, Viridian and his partners were reconciled to the idea and his concern had been groundless.

Instead of merely shaking hands, Viridian started to squeeze. He was a strong man, capable of exerting considerable force. That showed in the agonized expression which sprang to Dover's face.

Losing every suggestion of amiability, the burly man gave a tug and jerked Dover toward him. Even as the rancher opened his mouth to yell, Viridian continued with the attack. Clenching his left fist, he rammed it savagely into his captive's belly. All the breath rushed from Dover's lungs and pain caused him to double over. Snatching free his right hand, Viridian transferred it and his left to the rancher's shoulders. With a twisting heave, he hurled his victim backward to crash against the wall of the nearest building.

"Go and watch the street, Timson!" Viridian snapped, striding after Dover.

While the hardcase hurried away, Viridian brought up his right hand. Before the rancher could recover his wits and think of defending himself, he was caught by the throat. With the thumb and fingers sinking into his flesh, he was lifted erect and pinned against the wall. Moving in, Silvane plucked the revolver from Dover's holster and anticipated his weak, fumbling grab for it.

"So you're going to team up with some other small ranchers and take your cattle to Kansas, are you?" Viridian snarled, loosening his hold a trifle. "And whose idea is that?"

Hurt, dazed, and half-strangled, Dover could offer no resistance. He understood what was being said to him, but could not prevent the words which came boiling out.

"Yo—you—bast—" the rancher began, then tried to raise his voice. "Hel—!"

Clamping down his hold on the throat, Viridian propelled his left fist into Dover's belly for the second time. The word came to an abrupt halt, but the recipient of the blow was held upright and could not bend over in an attempt to relieve the pain.

"Try yelling again and see what you get," Viridian snarled, giving Dover's head a sharp rap against the wall and once more loosening but not removing his grasp on the throat. "You don't have the brains to think up that notion. So who told you about it?"

"F—Feller down to Mulcachy's livery barn," the rancher gasped, knowing the futility of refusing to answer or trying to resist. "I was just talking to him about it."

"Who is he?" Viridian demanded.

Wanting to decide how he might best answer, Dover did not reply immediately. He saw the anger increase on Viridian's face and felt the grip tightening about his throat, so spoke hurriedly. "A short-growed, blond-haired kid. I don't know his name."

"If you're lying—!" the burly man began.

"It's the truth!" Dover yelped. "He was only a kid, but he reckoned he'd been on the drive with Goodnight and had seen letters from the Eastern buyers."

"And you believed him?" Viridian challenged.

"No. I didn't take too much account of what he said."

"You didn't?"

"N—No. Hell. I don't reckon he'd've been more than a wrangler, or the cook's louse, even if he *had* been on the drive."

Watching his victim's face, Viridian was puzzled. There was something wrong, but he could not decide exactly what it might be. He doubted whether Dover would dare lie to him, especially about the source of the information when it could easily be checked on. Perhaps the rancher had given the story more credence than he had declared and was afraid of being found out. That might account for his attitude.

"If I find he wasn't who you say," Viridian snarled. "I'll cripple you!"

"Send one of your men to see," Dover countered. "The kid's the only one at the barn. Everybody else's gone to see the Governor open the Fair."

If the rancher was bluffing, Viridian decided that he was making a good job of it. So he decided to accept the story and go on with the main part of his business.

"Do you reckon you can sell cattle up in Kansas?" he asked.

"N—No," Dover replied and stiffened as if expecting the attack to be resumed.

Instead, Viridian removed his right hand and used it to extract some papers from his jacket's inside pocket. He separated one, opened it, and returned the rest. Crouching slightly and rubbing his stomach, Dover watched what was being done. Next the burly man produced a small writing case from the pocket.

"That being the case," Viridian said, flicking up the lid of the small ink pot in the container. "You'll be willing to sign this."

"Wh—What is it?" Dover wanted to know.

"A contract to deliver five hundred head of cattle to us every three months," Viridian replied.

"Fi—Five *hundred* head?" the rancher croaked.

"To be delivered every three months," Viridian repeated. "With a penalty clause of one third of their value for nondelivery."

"But—But—" Dover spluttered, realizing what signing the contract would mean. "I'd have to strip my range bare to keep up the deliveries."

"Look at it this way," Viridian replied. "You can't sell them anywhere else, except to another hide and tallow factory. Can you?"

"Well—" Dover began and saw the nib of the pen Viridian had removed from the case moving toward his face. "Well no, I—I can't."

"And we're increasing our price to *six* dollars a head," Viridian went on. "None of the other factories pays that high, does it?"

"No," the rancher conceded.

"Then this's a fair offer," Viridian stated. "Isn't it?"

"I—I—" Dover commenced, looking around in desperation.

Apart from the three men, there was not another human being in sight. Timson was standing at the mouth of the alley, watching the street without giving any indication that there were people about. Still holding Dover's revolver, Silvane had walked to the rear and was peering around the corner toward Mulcachy's livery barn. Although only Viridian was within reaching distance, Dover knew that he could not hope to escape in his present condition.

"Look at it this way," the burly man suggested, guessing at the thoughts that were running through the rancher's head. "You've told me that you don't believe there's a chance of selling your cattle in Kansas. So I'm offering you a good deal and a steady source of income. Why shouldn't you sign?"

"I—I'd like time to think about it."

"Time's one thing neither of us have. I've got other ranchers to see and they'll be willing to sign. So it's now or never."

"But—" Dover began, playing for time in the hope that the marshal or a deputy would make an appearance.

"This's how I see it," Viridian interrupted, scowling in a menacing manner. "Either you've told me the truth about Kansas, in which case there's no reason not to sign, or you've been lying to me. I don't like liars."

"What if I won't sign?" the rancher wanted to know.

"I'd like that a whole heap less," Viridian replied. "And

like you said, there's a lot of tough fellers in town for the Fair. If you was found with your head bust in and your pockets emptied, everybody'd think it was done in a robbery. I could always give your wife the same offer. But if I had to, the price would go down to *four* dollars."

"G—Give me the contract," Dover requested, knowing that he had not been threatened idly.

"You'll find it's legally binding," Viridian warned when the rancher had taken the pen and contract, but hesitated. "Don't get any clever notions like signing, then going to lay a complaint with the marshal. He'll not find me in town. And if he telegraphs Pilar, he'll be told that I'm at home, in bed with the grippe. Don't forget that you and your family have to go home. It's a long, lonely road. Anything could happen on it."

The final words had the desired effect. Dover had heard about and seen the pleasure Viridian took in slaughtering cattle. Such a man would have little regard for the sanctity of human life. So the rancher decided that he must comply and hope that, in the future, the law would give him its protection. With that thought, he affixed his signature to the document.

Guessing what his employer had in mind, Silvane had left him to deal with the rancher. In all probability Viridian would want to interview the "short-growed, blond-haired kid." So the hardcase had walked to the rear of the alley with the intention of checking if it could be done.

At first sight, the livery barn appeared to be devoid of human life. On the point of returning and telling Viridian that the rancher might have been lying, Silvane saw a figure leave the big main building and stroll in his direction. Although at least two hundred yards separated them, the hardcase could see that the approaching man answered to Dover's brief description. Withdrawing his head hurriedly and, as he believed, unobserved, Silvane strode back to his employer.

"Boss!" Silvane uttered. "That kid's just coming this way."

"He is, huh?" Viridian grunted, shaking the contract to dry the ink. He had already packed and put away the writing case. "Timson, come here!"

Hope began to well inside Dover. If the young man who had given the information was who he had claimed to be and—unlikely as it seemed—the rancher had believed him, there was a chance that he might still escape from his predicament. Opening his mouth to yell a warning, he lunged forward with the intention of grabbing and destroying the contract. Just an instant too late, he realized that Viridian had guessed what he was planning to do.

Having seen and understood the brief play of emotions on the rancher's face, the burly man was aware of what he had in mind. So he was ready to counter the attempt when it was made.

Snatching the contract clear of Dover's clutching fingers, Viridian advanced a pace. Coming into close proximity with the rancher, he swung up his bent right leg. Anger gave added impetus to what would have been a devastating attack and made it that much more effective. The knee passed between Dover's thighs and rammed against his testicles. Sudden, raw, and raging torment burst through him, a pain such as he had never experienced. Instead of shouting and drawing attention to his plight, he gave a croaking gasp. Jackknifing at the middle, with his hands flying involuntarily to the stricken region, he collapsed to his knees. Mouthing furious curses, Viridian kicked the all-but helpless man at the side of the head and he went sprawling limply onto his face.

"That ought to keep him quiet," Timson remarked callously, joining his employer. "What's up, boss?"

"We've got another one to see," Viridian answered, checking that the ink was dry before folding and returning the contract to his pocket. "Leave that gun, Silvane."

"Sure, boss," the hardcase answered and tossed the revolver down alongside its owner. "Are we going after that kid?"

"Yes," the burly man confirmed. "And by the time I get through with him, he's going to wish he'd never even heard of taking cattle to Kansas."

3
I KNOW *SOMETHING* ABOUT IT

Without as much as a glance at the unconscious rancher, Viridian led his men along the alley. He wanted to leave it before the "blond-haired kid" arrived and saw Dover. Stepping around the corner he found that he had achieved his ambition. The cowhand had covered slightly more than half of the distance from the livery barn and was still coming.

Studying his intended victim while walking forward, Viridian decided that Dover's description had been very apt. What was more, he doubted if he would have any difficulty in persuading the young cowhand to stop talking about taking herds to Kansas.

Not more than five feet six inches from his low-crowned, wide-brimmed black Stetson to his high-heeled, fancy-stitched boots, the cowhand seemed short and insignificant. He had curly, dusty blond hair and a tanned, fairly good-looking set of features. While his clothing seemed to be of good quality, it bore the marks of long travel. He made the tight-rolled scarlet bandanna, black and white calf skin vest, gray shirt and jeans, their cuffs hanging outside his boots and turned back, look like somebody else's castoffs.

Strangely enough, considering his profession, Silvane

had not commented on the fact that the blond was armed. Viridian noticed the brown leather gun belt, with two white-handled Colt 1860 Army revolvers in carefully designed cross-draw holsters, but discounted them. If the cowhand had ridden on Goodnight's drive, even in the menial capacity of horse wrangler or cook's assistance, he would have been paid well enough to be able to afford such an excellent gun-rig. Most likely he had purchased it in an attempt to add to his stature.

If Viridian had been more observant, he might have noticed that the cowhand had a good width to his shoulders and trimmed down at the waist in a manner suggestive of strength. Also, he walked without any hint of a swagger such as an insignificant youngster might adopt when trying to appear tough.

Fanning out and allowing Viridian to draw ahead of them, Timson and Silvane also examined the small Texan. While they took note of his weapons, neither felt any concern. If their employer used the same trick that he had played upon the rancher, the cowhand would not have an opportunity to defend himself.

"Howdy," greeted Viridian, trying to sound like a Texan and coming to a halt directly in front of the blond. "You-all the young feller's knows all about taking herds to Kansas?"

"I know *something* about it," the cowhand corrected, his voice pleasant and suggesting that he had had a good education. At the same time, his gray eyes flickered from Viridian to the two hardcases. To avoid alarming him or arousing his suspicions, Timson and Silvane had stopped several feet away. Apparently they had succeeded, for he returned his gaze to their employer. "Are you interested, mister?"

"Why sure," Viridian agreed. "We ride for the Walking O, up Wise County way, and the boss's in town to find out what it's all about."

On the burly man mentioning the ranch at which he was

supposed to work, the blond glanced down at his hands and to the Hersome gaiter boots.

"He'll find out easy enough," the youngster said, resuming his scrutiny of Viridian's face. "All he has to do is come to the Convention."

"*You* figure it can be done, huh?" Viridian inquired, noticing that the blond's reply implied he would be attending the Convention. That could not be. The meeting was for the owners of ranches, or their representatives. It seemed highly unlikely that he came into either category.

"Sure," the blond answered evenly. "I figure it can."

Watching and listening, Viridian decided that he did not like the way in which the blond was acting. There was none of the bombast and posturing that were usually evident when an insignificant nobody was trying to act like a man of importance. Rather he seemed to exude quiet confidence. What was more, he gave the impression that he knew what he was talking about and would repay being listened to. That was all the more reason for silencing him. He might be capable of persuading unconvinced ranchers to attend the Convention.

There was another point for Viridian to take into consideration. If the suggestion had come from the blond that Dover should share the expenses of a trail drive with the owners of other small ranches, he must be smarter than he looked. Certainly it was not a notion that Viridian wanted passed around.

"The boss'll be right pleased to hear it," Viridian declared, looking around. Nobody was watching, so he could go ahead with his plan and there would be no interruptions. Adopting a jovially disarming attitude, he thrust forward his right hand. "The name's Doug Wright—"

"Pleased to meet you," the blond drawled. Standing apparently relaxed and at ease, he seemed to be falling into the trap.

Still grinning in a friendly fashion, Viridian prepared to close his fingers around, and grasp the offered hand, with all his crushing pressure. Even if the blond wanted to, pain would prevent him from trying to draw a revolver.

However, before the burly man's scheme could be implemented, the young cowhand showed that he had not been fooled by the other's words or actions. Instead, he was clearly aware of the danger.

As their palms came into contact, the relaxation left the Texan and he began to move with commendable speed. Before Viridian realized what was happening, the Texan's right thumb was pressing on the back of his hand and turning it palm downward. At the same instant, the blond's left hand flashed up to cup under and grasp the burly man's right elbow. There was surprising strength in the youngster's grip. It showed in the ease with which he raised the trapped forearm and bent the wrist forward with a whip-like, snapping motion. Such was the pain caused by the hold that Viridian was effectively prevented from continuing with his attack.

Seeing that their boss was not duplicating the success he had had with the rancher, Silvane and Timson moved forward to help him. Being closer than his companion, Silvane arrived first. He went by Viridian from the left, hoping to take the Texan by surprise.

The hope did not materialize.

Still retaining his painful wristlock on the burly man, the blond stepped swiftly to his right. So fast did he move that Viridian could do nothing to prevent him. Up whipped his right leg, driving the toe of his boot with equal precision and at the same target that Viridian had put his knee into when felling the rancher. And with just as much success. Letting out a gasping cry, Silvane lost all interest in making the attack. Instead, he blundered by a couple of steps and bent double. Then he tumbled onto his face and lay writhing in agony. It was obvious that he would not be getting up for some minutes.

Viridian had been dragged around so that he was between the Texan and Timson. Spluttering anguished curses, the burly man swung his left fist toward his captor. Due to the awkwardness and pain of the hold upon him, he could not deliver a really effective blow. However, passing beneath the brim of the Stetson, his knuckles collided with the blond's cheek. Although the punch was not as hard as it would have been in more favorable circumstances, it served its purpose. Or, perhaps, the blond had already planned to release the wrist. Whichever it was, Viridian found himself liberated. But not before the cowhand had given a sharp, downward jerk at the trapped hand. An added agony ripped into Viridian and he thought for a moment that his wrist had been broken, or at least sprained.

Giving the burly man no chance to recover and follow up the blow, the cowhand sprang to his left. Swerving around his employer, Timson appeared before the blond. If the youngster was surprised or perturbed by finding himself confronted by another enemy, he did not show any sign of it. Lunging forward, Timson cut loose with a haymaker of a right hand punch. Going under the hardcase's fist, the blond flung a much more scientific left jab into his unguarded belly. The knuckles sank home with all the power of a muscular frame behind them. Giving a grunt that was testimony to the force of the blow, Timson changed his attack into an involuntary retreat. To his horror, he saw that the blond did not intend to let him go unhindered. Like a flash, the youngster struck with his left fist and it rose in the direction of the hardcase's descending jaw.

Brief as it had been, the respite allowed Viridian to recover from the effect of the wristlock. Shaking his right hand, he concluded that he had been premature in diagnosing the extent of the injury. While his wrist throbbed sorely, it was neither broken nor sprained. Satisfied on that point, he turned his attention toward obtaining revenge on his assailant. Stepping forward while the blond was occupied with Timson, Viridian reached out with his right hand.

He had decided that, as his wrist was still aching, he would be able to punch more effectively with his left hand.

With his hand rising toward its target, the blond felt his shirt's collar seized from the rear. Taken by surprise, his torso was bent backward. While the attack did not entirely save Timson, it reduced the power of the blow to his jaw. Lifted erect by the impact, the hardcase reeled a few steps, but he did not go down.

Once again, the youngster displayed a keen appreciation of his danger. It was the burly man's intention to jerk him off balance and either throw him to the ground, or smash home blows with the left hand. But the youngster proved himself capable of producing an effective counter to the attack.

Retaining his balance as best he could, the blond swung his right foot in a circle to the rear. That brought his back and right shoulder so they pressed against Viridian's right elbow and prevented him from exerting the pull to any greater degree. With that done, the cowhand glanced down. Having located his target, he raised and stamped his right foot backward. His aim was very good. The high heel of the boot caught Viridian on the front of the shin bone. Yelling in pain, the burly man released his hold and turned to the left. Pivoting fast, the blond drove his bent right arm so that its elbow caught Viridian in the kidney region. Grunting in agony, the man stumbled away from his assailant.

Timson was back into the attack. Leaping in as the blond's elbow struck his employer, the hardcase caught him by the other arm. A sharp tug turned the youngster, followed by a punch into his stomach. Releasing the biceps, having been surprised by the discovery of its bulk, Timson followed the blow with another to the same area. Although the Texan grunted and was forced backward, he had had time to brace his powerful stomach muscles and reduce the effect of the blows. Following him, the hardcase changed the point of attack. Instead of punching, Timson shot out

his hands to grab hold on either side of the blond's throat
with the intention of choking him insensible.

Throwing a glance at his employer, as he secured his
grip, Timson decided that there would not be any immediate help from that source. Rubbing a hand on his back,
where the blond's elbow had landed, he was just stopping
but had not turned. His attitude suggested that he was in
some pain. Nor was Silvane in any better condition to lend
a hand. Still lying on the ground, he was in a crouching
posture and moaning piteously.

Even before the strangulation could start to take effect,
the blond moved to counteract it. Taking a long stride to
the rear with his right foot, he crouched slightly and caused
his attacker's torso to be inclined in his direction. Then he
placed the palms of his hands together, with the fingers
pointing into the air, but kept his elbows spread apart.
Thrusting his hands between Timson's arms, as the hardcase attempted to draw them both into a more upright
posture, the blond slid his left boot until it was level with
his right foot. Helped by his weight dragging on the clutching hands, the Texan's elbows forced open Timson's arms
and caused him to lose his hold.

Thrown off balance, the hardcase stumbled forward. At
the same moment, the blond snapped up a kick with his
right foot. Once again Timson might have counted himself
fortunate that circumstances prevented an attack from arriving with his opponent's full strength. As it was, the rapidly delivered kick still inflicted considerable pain. Caught
in the groin as he advanced, Timson was hurt but not incapacitated. Nor could he stop himself from blundering onward. The cowhand sidestepped, meaning to launch a blow
that would put his second enemy out of the deal.

Then the blond's luck started to go bad!

Viridian had turned and was closing in fast. Even as the
youngster moved clear of Timson, the burly man was in
striking distance. Hurling out his knotted left fist, Viridian
caught the blond in the solar plexus. Well-developed

though the Texan's stomach muscles were, they could not fend off such a blow. Gasping, he bent at the waist. He was winded and helpless.

Leaping closer, as his victim was driven to the rear by the impact, Viridian flung up his right knee. Although he overshot his mark, catching the blond's chest instead of the face, the result was equally satisfactory. Lifted erect, the blond was pitched bodily away from his attacker. Going by Timson, the cowhand smashed into the wall of the building and bounced limply to the ground.

"The bastard!" Timson screeched, left hand clutching between his thighs in an attempt to lessen the pain he was feeling. His right clawed the revolver from its holster. "I'll kill him!"

Even as the hardcase started to line his weapon, it became apparent that good fortune had not entirely deserted the now defenseless cowhand.

"Hey!" yelled a voice.

Turning to see who had shouted, Viridian realized that the situation was taking a turn for the worse. In fact, he might find himself in a dangerous predicament. Two men had emerged from an alley something over fifty yards away and were taking an undesirable interest in his affairs. What was more, they looked like they would be capable of backing up their intervention.

Both wore range clothes and the vest of the older, slightly shorter—which did not make him small—newcomer carried a deputy town marshal's shield. His right hand was dipping toward the butt of the revolver in the holster tied to his thigh.

Clad in all-black garments, with a gun belt that supported a heavy Colt—possibly even a Dragoon model— butt forward in a low cavalry-twist-draw holster at the right side and an ivory-handled bowie knife sheathed on the left, the second intruder gave the impression of being very young. He had an Indian-dark face that was handsome and almost babyishly innocent of aspect. If he too was a peace officer, he did not wear a badge to prove it.

For all the lack of evidence to suggest official status, Viridian considered the black-dressed cowhand to present the more immediate danger. He was already swinging toward his right shoulder the butt of the rifle that had been on the crook of his left arm. Young and innocent he might look, but he was moving with a speed and precision that implied he was very proficient in the use of the weapon.

Also having directed his gaze to the speaker, Timson snarled a curse and rapidly altered his point of aim. Elevating the barrel of his revolver, he squeezed its trigger. He made a lucky, or—depending upon how one looked at it—unlucky, hit. Although he had intended to shoot the black-dressed cowhand, his .44 caliber bullet struck the deputy in the chest. An instant later, flame spurted from the muzzle of the cowhand's rifle. Timson's head snapped back. He had lost his hat during the fight and the base of his skull seemed to shatter outward as the bullet burst its way through.

Anger, mingled with alarm, filled Viridian as he saw the result of Timson's shot. While the burly man had drawn his Remington instinctively, he had not intended to use it. Instead, he had hoped that he might be able to explain the position in a way which would satisfy the peace officer. Timson's action had ruined any chance of that.

One thing was now obvious to the hide and tallow man. He must get away as quickly as possible. Doing so would not be easy. The Indian-dark Texan's right hand was dipping in a significant manner. Taken with the second tube, beneath the barrel, the action implied that he held a Henry repeating rifle and could recharge its chamber with some rapidity.

Swinging on his heel to take a hurried departure, Viridian saw Silvane. The hardcase was slowly heaving himself onto his hands and knees, raising an ashy-gray, agony-distorted face to stare about him. Clearly he could not hope to escape in his present physical condition. Realizing that, Viridian did not like the idea of letting him fall into the hands of the law. The marshal would not be content with only two of the men concerned in the death of his deputy, but was going to want to know the identity of the third.

Having no faith in Silvane's loyalty, Viridian knew what he must do. Extending his right arm, he pointed the Remington downward. Horror twisted at the hardcase's face as he realized what his employer intended to do. Even as he opened his mouth, meaning to plead for his life, the revolver's hammer fell and a .36 conical-shaped lead ball twirled from the barrel into his head.

Almost before Silvane's lifeless body had jerked and fallen facedown, Viridian was racing by. Chancing a glance over his shoulder, the burly man saw that the black-dressed Texan was looking at the deputy. Sprinting on, Viridian swerved toward the alley. It was fortunate that he did. With an eerie crack, something struck and tore the hat from his head. Hearing the bark of the Texan's rifle, he knew what had happened.

Coming to a halt at the entrance to the alley, the burly man swiveled around. He raised the Remington, cupping his left hand under the right for added support, sighted, and fired. For a moment, he thought that he had scored a hit. The Texan plunged forward, but he went down in a rolling dive that showed he was not hurt. That was made even more certain by the way he came to his knees and started to return the rifle to the firing position.

Without waiting to see any more, Viridian resumed his flight. The sight of Dover sprawling before him gave a warning that there was another person who could identify him by name. Showing no more compassion than when slaughtering cattle, he flung a shot at the rancher. Dirt erupted alongside Dover's body, warning that the bullet had missed. Striding closer, Viridian bent and placed the muzzle of the revolver against the rancher's head. He had already cocked the action and, on squeezing the trigger, there was a smell of burning hair and flesh. Satisfied that he had silenced Dover, he flung himself onward.

Expecting at any moment to hear, or feel, something to prove that the dark-faced Texan had arrived at the other end of the alley, Viridian reached the street. Neither a shout nor a shot had followed him, so he assumed that the cowhand had stopped to examine one or another of the injured men. So far, too, the shooting did not appear to have aroused any attention in the immediate neighborhood.

Having seen Dover in passing, Viridian and his men had hitched their horses in front of the right-hand building. Darting to them, he started to jerk free the reins of Silvane's mount. Muttering a relieved curse, he felt he was fortunate that the hardcases each used one-piece reins instead of the split-ended, two brand variety preferred by Texas cowhands. Tossing the reins over the saddle's horn, he repeated the process with Timson's horse. Then he liberated and vaulted astride his own animal. Reining it around, he yelled to set the other two running. They could not be traced back to him if the peace officers caught them, but he had no intention of leaving them to be used by the Texan. From what he had seen, the Indian-dark youngster was too skilled a fighting man for him to be inclined to take chances of that kind.

With Timson's and Silvane's mounts running along the street, Viridian set his horse into motion. Building up its speed, he guided it at an angle and into an alley on the other side of the street. As he entered, he flung a fast look behind him. So far, the Texan had not made an appearance. With the horse going at a gallop, Viridian made his way to the edge of the town. Once there, he joined the stagecoach trail, knowing that it would be difficult, if not impossible, for anybody to follow his horse's tracks along it.

Riding on, keeping a wary watch for pursuit, Viridian gave thought to what he should do next. He decided that he would return that night, after dark, and consult with de Froissart. There were other men in town who he could use and he might be able to carry out his task despite the setback.

Thinking of the latter subject, Viridian scowled. He wondered who the "short-growed, blond-haired kid" might be?

4

DO YOU KNOW WHO
THAT *KID* IS?

To the north of Fort Worth, rockets hissed into the sky and
exploded with brilliant cascades of multicolored lights. The
red glows of several large fires in the same direction told
that the open-air barbecue to celebrate the commence-
ment of the Tarrant County Fair was in full swing.

Holding his horse to a walk, Austin Viridian ignored the
festivities and rode toward the Belle Grande Hotel. The
time was shortly after ten o'clock and the night dark. None
of the few people on the street gave him a second glance as
he went by. There were so many strangers in town that one
more attracted no attention, especially when he was behav-
ing in a normal manner. So, although he remained con-
stantly on the alert and continually darted glances about
him, it was merely an instinctive precautionary measure.
He did not believe that he would be connected with the
killings of that afternoon. In fact, such was the change in
his appearance, that he felt sure neither the small blond
nor the Indian-dark cowhand would recognize him if they
should happen to meet.

After having covered about two miles along the south-
bound stagecoach trail, without seeing anybody coming after him, Viridian had turned off it across some bare and
rocky ground which would not show his horse's tracks. He

had made his way to a grove of post oak trees and, finding a small stream, had made his preparations for going back to town.

Prudence might have suggested that the burly man had kept riding until he gained the safety of Pilar, but he had wanted to find out what was happening in Fort Worth. De Froissart had reached the town shortly after noon and, guessing that Viridian was involved in the shootings, would have tried to discover what progress—if any—the marshal was making in the investigation. Rather than wait at home until the Creole brought or sent the information, Viridian intended to hear it as soon as possible.

There was another reason for Viridian returning. Timson and Silvane were dead, but he could replace them without difficulty. Of course, he would not be able to carry out his work as had been planned originally. For all that, he was satisfied that he could revise the scheme for persuading ranchers to continue supplying the Pilar Hide & Tallow Company with cattle.

The first thing Viridian had had to do was alter his appearance. That had been easy enough to accomplish. In the bedroll strapped to the cantle of his saddle had been his more usual style of clothing, with the exception of his "planter's" hat. He had not been able to carry that, but did not think its absence was important. Unpacking the bedroll, he had stripped off the cowhand's attire. He had washed and shaved in the cold water of the stream although doing so had been painful. He had had no means of heating any water. Then, having dressed as he did normally and looking more respectable, he had waited with what patience he could muster until night had fallen. There had been no sign of a posse searching for him and, with the coming of the darkness, his worries on that account had ended.

On his return, Viridian had found—as he had expected —that the southern side of the town was still practically deserted. Nor had there been many people around as he had ridden through the more wealthy section toward the hotel which he and his partners always used when visiting Fort Worth. He wanted to make sure that de Froissart had arrived before wasting time in searching for him.

Fastening his horse to the hotel's hitching rail, the burly man strolled across the sidewalk in a deliberately nonchalant manner. Caution dictated that he should try to see his partner and learn the situation before meeting anybody else who knew him. So he looked through the open front door. He was gratified to find the lobby and the reception desk unoccupied.

Entering, Viridian made the most of his opportunity by crossing to the desk and examining the register. At the top of a fresh page, its first entry in fact, was his partner's name. Glancing at the keyboard, he saw that de Froissart's key was missing.

Annoyance bit at the burly man. Instead of being out and attending to the Company's business, the Creole must be having an early night in bed. Maybe he was tired after the journey from Pilar, but he ought to be learning all he could about the extent of the peace officers' investigation into the killings. Nor was it like him to miss a celebration like the barbecue, especially when it offered the chance of meeting influential and useful people.

Sniffing indignantly, Viridian went upstairs. He met nobody, nor did he have any difficulty in locating de Froissart's room. At first, as no light showed through the crack at the bottom of the door, he wondered if the Creole had taken the key with him instead of handing it in at the desk. Drawing closer, he could faintly hear voices. While he could not make out what was being said, or even tell for sure that it was de Froissart, he decided that a man and woman were talking.

The discovery did not come as too much of a surprise to Viridian, for the Creole fancied himself as a ladies' man. It accounted for him being in his room at such an early hour —and did nothing to reduce the burly man's annoyance.

However, not wishing to stand in the passage for too long and feeling satisfaction at being able to spoil de Froissart's fun, he knocked on the door.

"Who is it?" called the Creole's voice, sounding annoyed.

"Gus Roxterby," Viridian answered, taking the precaution in case anybody else should hear him. He was confident that his partner would recognize his voice. "Open up, Mr. de—!"

Before the burly man could say anything more, there was a loud and clearly startled exclamation from the Creole. It was followed by a brief, much quieter mutter of conversation between de Froissart and his companion. Viridian could not hear what was being said, but guessed that his partner was explaining matters to the woman. Then, partially muffled by de Froissart calling that he was coming, Viridian heard a scuffling sound as if somebody was moving hurriedly but attempting to do so without making too much noise.

Despite the Creole's promise, several seconds elapsed before Viridian saw a glow of light under the door and heard footsteps approaching. The lock clicked and the door opened to reveal de Froissart. He was wearing a woolen dressing gown, but little else. There was surprise, mingled with alarm, on his handsome face and he kept his right hand hidden behind the door.

"What are you doing he—" the Creole began.

"What took you so long?" Viridian inquired, in the same breath.

"I—You woke me up," de Froissart replied, darting a glance over his shoulder. "And I had to light the lamp, then put this on. But why—?"

"Let's talk inside," Viridian suggested, stepping forward. "It'd be best if nobody knows I'm in town."

"That's true enough," de Froissart admitted and his eyes held a wary look. "Why *did* you come back?"

"To find out what's being done about this afternoon," Viridian answered, continuing to advance.

"Is that a—" the Creole said, sounding relieved and taking another look behind him. Most of the alarm had gone when he returned his gaze to his partner. Letting the burly man walk by, he closed the door. "It might have been wiser if you'd stayed away."

Looking about him, Viridian could locate no trace of de Froissart's other visitor. For a moment, he wondered if he had been imagining the female voice. Then his nostrils detected a sweet, somehow familiar aroma and he grinned. Unless he was mistaken, the woman had on the same kind of expensive perfume his wife always used. There was no wonder that the Creole had not wanted Viridian to see her, or even suspect she was there. In all probability, she was an ostensibly respectable married woman with a wealthy husband. Possibly Viridian was acquainted with her.

Most likely, the burly man thought as he continued his examination of the room, the woman was now standing inside the large wardrobe. It was the only possible hiding place and, apart from going through the window, there was no other way out.

She certainly would not have crawled under the bed, Viridian decided as he swung his gaze in that direction, although she had been in it. The covers were thrown back, while the mattress and one pillow showed plainly that more than a single person had been pressing on them.

Wondering if he could learn the woman's identity as a means of getting a hold over his partner, Viridian noticed that de Froissart's walking-cane was lying on the bed. Yet it looked different in some way. After a moment's scrutiny, he realized what was wrong.

The cane's handle was missing!

Turning slowly, Viridian dropped his gaze to the Creole's right hand. It was gripping the sword portion of the walking-cane.

"What's that for?" the burly man asked, indicating the weapon.

At the same time, moving in an apparently casual manner, Viridian's left hand unbuttoned his jacket. By doing so, he gave access to the butt of his Remington if it should be needed, but avoided making his intentions too obvious. Taking in his action, de Froissart made no references to it. Instead, the Creole strolled in what could have been a genuinely nonchalant manner until he stood between Viridian and the wardrobe. Although near to the bed, on the opposite side to where he and the woman had been lying, de Froissart did not offer to return the sword to its sheath in the cane.

"I wasn't sure who was outside," the Creole answered.

"Didn't you recognize my voice?" Viridian challenged.

"Well, yes, but I could hardly believe it was you speaking," de Froissart replied. "Why have you come back, Austin?"

"Have I been here before?" Viridian countered.

The burly man was puzzled by his partner's attitude. Displaying agitation, the Creole repeatedly flickered nervous glances over his shoulder at the wardrobe. Viridian considered saying that it was nothing to him if de Froissart chose to entertain a woman, but decided against it. Wanting information, he had no desire to antagonize the Creole and any reference to the other's bed mate was sure to do that.

"Not that I know of," de Froissart said quietly. "And, if you know what's good for you, you'll not be here after midnight."

"Why not?" Viridian challenged, eyeing the Creole suspiciously.

"If you stay in town," de Froissart warned, "you could find yourself in more trouble than you can handle."

"How do you mean?"

"You might be recognized from this afternoon's affair."

"Only that damned short-grown kid saw me close

enough for that and, even if he did recognize me, who'd take *his* word against mine?"

"Do you know who that *kid* is?" de Froissart inquired, staring straight into his partner's beefy face and no longer paying any attention to the wardrobe.

"Just a cowhand—" Viridian began.

"Just a cowhand!" de Froissart blurted.

"If he was that," Viridian went on, puzzled by the Creole's behavior.

"If he was *only* that," de Froissart corrected. "Austin. He is Dusty Fog!"

"Dusty Fog?" the burly man repeated.

"You must have heard of him," the Creole declared.

"Of course I have," Viridian snorted. "According to these beef-head bastards, he nearly made the North lose the War single-handed in Ark—" Then understanding came and brought the words to a stop. When he spoke again, his voice held a disbelieving note. "Are you trying to tell me that that runty son of a bitch is *Dusty Fog?"*

"He is," de Froissart confirmed.

"Somebody must have been joshing you!" Viridian declared, despite the obvious sincerity in the Creole's voice. "He *couldn't* be Dusty Fog."

There was good reason for the burly man's reaction. The name he had been given was one to conjure with in Texas. Thinking of the blond, Viridian could hardly credit that such a small, insignificant youngster was the already almost legendary Dusty Fog.[1]

"Harlow Dolman wouldn't joke about anything *that* important," de Froissart warned.

"Harlow Dolman!" Viridian spat out and the two words were redolent of suspicion. "How does he get mixed in this?"

"He came with us."

1. New readers can find further details of Dusty Fog's career in Appendix 1.

"Us?"

"One of his men arrived with a message for him and I let them share the coach," de Froissart explained. "And it's lucky that he did come. He told me all he knew before he took the posse out to hunt for you."

"He took the posse after me?" Viridian growled.

"With the letters, we thought it would be better to have somebody who *wouldn't* try to catch you," de Froissart pointed out.

"I thought they'd come in useful," the burly man commented dryly.

Before leaving Pilar, Viridian had insisted upon having his partners' concurrence with his intentions put into writing. There had been some acrimonious debate over the suggestion, but he had been adamant. As the share of any partner who died reverted to the surviving members, and because he would be taking all the chances, he had insisted upon having some form of protection. It would also guarantee the other three's support if things went wrong. Yielding to the demand, his wife, Schweitzer, de Froissart, and Profaci had signed the documents, with Harlow Dolman as a witness. While his partners had retained one copy each, Viridian had demanded that he be given two.

"Where are your copies?" de Froissart inquired worriedly.

"In good hands, like I said they'd be," Viridian replied. "And he knows what to do with them, if I should meet with any accidents."

"I thought trust in each other was the basis of any partnership!" de Froissart said, with real, or assumed, indignation.

"It is," Viridian answered, then decided to revert to the subject which had brought him to the hotel. "So Dolman's out hunting for me?"

"Yes. And it's lucky for you that he was here. If he hadn't been, Marshal Grillman would have been leading the posse. At that, I doubt if Grillman would have agreed to let Dolman go if his deputy had been killed instead of just wounded. As it was, it still took the Governor to persuade him to stay and look after the town."

"That was lucky," Viridian conceded.

"Luckier than you know," de Froissart stated. "If Grillman had gone after you, he'd have had somebody capable of finding you. And who was ready to do it after what you'd done to his friends."

"How do you mean?"

"You've heard of the Ysabel Kid?"

"I've heard of him. How does he come into it?"

"He rides for the OD Connected, Fog's ranch, now," de Froissart explained and, try as he might, he could not prevent a trace of malicious delight from entering his voice as he watched Viridian's expression change to one of alarm. "And he was with the deputy you shot."

"If he says I shot the deputy, he's a liar!" Viridian barked, forgetting that his words were being overheard by the woman in the wardrobe. "Timson did it, not me."

Remembering various stories he had heard about the Ysabel Kid, Viridian felt as if an icy hand was pressing against his spine. Clearly he had had an even narrower escape than he had previously imagined. What was more, de Froissart had made a very good point. If only a fraction of the tales about the Ysabel Kid were true, Viridian did not want to be hunted by him. Particularly when he was angry over an attack upon one friend and the killing—or merely wounding—of another. With his background, upbringing, and education, the Ysabel Kid would be a very dangerous enemy.[2]

"Well, anyway, only Fog saw me close up," Viridian continued, after a few seconds' pause. "And he thinks I'm a Texas cowhand—"

"Don't count on it," de Froissart put in. "Harlow said that Fog had given him a good description, down to your

2. Details of these are given in Appendix 2.

Hersome gaiter boots and the Remington in your cross-draw holster. Your accent didn't fool him either. He knew you were neither a Texan nor a cowhand."

"How?"

"Like I said, by your accent. You tried to sound like a Texan, but didn't come close to succeeding. And cowhands don't wear flat-heeled boots. On top of that, he'd seen one of your men peeking at him from an alley."

Anger brought a deeper red flush to the burly man's cheeks. While he had believed that his deception had been successful, although its result was unlucky, he saw now that he was wrong. Dusty Fog—if it was him—had already been made suspicious and was prepared to defend himself from the beginning.

Not wanting to meet his partner's eyes until he had composed himself, Viridian dropped his gaze to the floor. Something gray showed from under the bed. A closer examination showed it to be the sleeve of a woman's Balmoral traveling coat. She was not wearing it, but must have thrust all her discarded garments beneath the bed before entering the wardrobe. Having been in a hurry, she had not noticed that the sleeve was protruding.

"Fog even told Harlow that, as you'd lost your hat, he should watch out for a bare-headed man," the Creole went on. He indicated a chair which stood by the bed. "You'd better borrow mine and wear it when you leave."

"Thanks," Viridian answered and went to pick up the white "planter's" hat. "I'd best be moving on."

"Where will you go?" de Froissart asked.

"Back to Pilar," the burly man replied. "If I see Roxterby on my way out, I'll tell him to keep the men doing their part. If I don't, you can see to it."

"I will," the Creole promised. "But I think we'd better forget about trying to make ranchers sign the contracts."

"And me," Viridian admitted. "Damn the luck. I'd made Dover sign one. We can't use it now."

"No," de Froissart agreed. "Do you want to leave it with me?"

"I'll burn it on the way home," Viridian decided, realizing what a damning piece of evidence the contract would be. Walking to the door, he drew it open and looked out to make sure he could leave unobserved. Satisfied, he glanced at his partner. "I'll see you back home, Pierre."

A thought struck Viridian as he was approaching the stairs. He had just taken part in a most indiscreet conversation, with an unknown woman able to hear every word of it. De Froissart must have a whole heap of faith and trust in his female visitor to have discussed the shootings and their aftermath so frankly. Whoever she might be, she now knew plenty that ought to have remained a secret between the partners.

Although Viridian tried to comfort himself with the thought that de Froissart knew what he was doing, the concern and uncertainty continued. He wondered who the woman was. The perfume had implied that she was well-to-do and the fact that she had hidden suggested she might be married. So, if he could discover her identity, he would have a hold over her which ought to ensure her silence. Perhaps she and her husband were staying at the hotel, and so she was taking advantage of his absence to carry out the clandestine meeting with the Creole. In which case, Viridian might be able to learn who she was from the register.

The lobby was still deserted and the burly man returned to the desk. He turned the left side page and looked at the names on it. Glancing down the lines, he sought for a clue—

And found it!

The final entry on the page, which must have been written just before de Froissart's, read, "Mrs. M. Viridian, Pilar, Falls County, Texas."

5

SEE THEY DON'T GET HOME ALIVE

At about the same time that Viridian was greeting de Froissart, the Ysabel Kid was walking across the barroom of the Post Oaks Saloon. He acknowledged the greetings of the four middle-aged men in range clothes who were seated around the table nearest to the counter.

Having noticed the quartet while passing the saloon, he had entered in the hope that they might wish to discuss the matter which had brought him to Fort Worth. It seemed likely that they might. He knew only one of them and had seen the man surreptitiously informing the others of his identity. However, he decided that it would be good policy to let them start the conversation.

"Beer, friend," the Kid requested, laying his rifle on the counter as the solitary bartender came toward him. Although it was still known as the "New, Improved" Henry, the weapon would soon be given the name by which it would become famous: the Winchester Model of 1866. "Take something for yourself."

"*Gracias,*" the bartender replied, studying the newcomer and drawing conclusions from what he saw. "I'll have me the same."

Normally the bartender would have stated that, even though nobody else was using it, his well-polished counter was not a repository for rifles; although he would not have phrased the complaint in those exact words. While tough and usually capable of enforcing his wishes, his scrutiny had warned him that here was a man who could not be taken lightly. Those red-hazel eyes gave a warning that the almost babyishly innocent aspect of the Indian-dark features was no more than skin deep. Underneath the surface lay a real hard *hombre*, with gravel in his guts and sand to burn. Maybe the old, walnut-handled Colt Second Model Dragoon revolver and the ivory-hilted bowie knife—which looked like it would have come from the birthplace of the original, old James Black's Arkansas forge—might have struck some folks as being just for show. Not so the bartender. He figured their owner would be mighty competent in using them, or the rifle.

Except for one detail of his all-black clothing, the Kid looked a typical Texas cowhand. However, his duties as a member of the OD Connected ranch's floating outfit[1] were chiefly concerned with scouting. A fair amount of such work had to be done on foot. So his boots had low heels, which allowed him an extra mobility and agility that could be important for keeping him alive.

"Hey, Kid," called the tallest of the seated quartet. "Do you reckon that Colonel Charlie's notion'll work?"

Turning so that the rifle was at his left side, the Kid rested his elbows on the counter and leaned against it. To his West-wise eyes, every man at the table was a top hand in the cattle industry. The speaker was foreman of a large ranch and the Kid guessed that the other three held similar positions. Having been told of the Kid's connection with Colonel Goodnight's trail drive, they were eager to hear his views on the subject. Which was quite a compliment, coming from men of their caliber. Being aware that their opinions would weigh heavily with their employers, he was

1. The term "floating outfit" is explained for new readers in Appendix 2.

determined to convince them that Goodnight's scheme was feasible.

"Why sure," the Kid replied, his voice a pleasant tenor drawl. "I reckon it will. We got that three thousand head to Fort Sumner without too much trouble."

"That's nowheres near's far as taking 'em to Kansas," the shortest of the four—a man of around five foot eleven —pointed out.

"Nope," the Kid agreed. "But there's nothing near's bad as the *Llano Estacado* to cross between here 'n' Kansas."

Although the Kid did not realize it, he had been followed to the saloon and hostile ears were taking in what was being said.

Standing outside the batwing doors, Gus Roxterby exchanged glances with his three companions.

"This's what we've been paid to stop," the factory supervisor informed them.

None of the three were aware of Roxterby's connection with the Pilar Hide & Tallow Company. Like others of their kind, they had drifted into Fort Worth hoping to find easy pickings at the Tarrant County Fair. While two of them were dressed like North Texas cowhands, neither had ever worked cattle on a ranch. They made their living with the revolvers in the tied-down holsters on their right thighs. One was young, brash-looking, fairly handsome, and dandified in a cheap, garish fashion. Older, the other was slightly shorter and took less care with his appearance.

The third man was tall, lean, with lank black hair and a somewhat aquiline, dark brown face that suggested a fair proportion of Indian blood. That impression was intensified by the eagle feather in the band of his high-crowned, dirty black hat, greasy buckskin shirt and trousers and Comanche moccasins. A tomahawk hung in the slings on the left side of his waist belt, being balanced by an 1860 Army Colt in a cavalry holster, from which the flap had been removed, at the right. His age would be somewhere between that of his two companions.

"Shouldn't be too hard to do," commented the youngest of the three, adopting a tone which he felt sure emphasized his salty, uncurried toughness. "Let's go to doing it."

Roxterby waited for the other two's objections to the statement. Older and more experienced than Jear Abbot, Si Wolkonski and *Nemenuh* Grift might consider that their task could prove more dangerous than he imagined. However, they were natives of North Texas and apparently did not recognize their potential victim.

That did *not* apply to Roxterby. He *knew* who they would be going up against.

Having accompanied Viridian to Fort Worth and been responsible for hiring the men, Roxterby had made it his business to learn all he could about the killings. He had been motivated by a desire to find out if he might be implicated in any way. Satisfied that he could not, he had contacted de Froissart and was told to continue with his work. Forcing ranchers to sign contracts was not his concern. He had to try to prevent rumors of the Kansas markets from being spread and accepted.

Selecting the trio, having known Grift and Wolkonski before he had taken up his present employment, he had been drifting around town without much hope of achieving anything. Most people were attending the barbecue and attempts at doing his work there were unlikely to be successful. The marshal and most of his deputies would be around, ready to prevent the disturbances and untoward incidents.

Seeing and identifying the Ysabel Kid, Roxterby had decided to follow him. After the part he had played that afternoon, Viridian would be pleased if something should happen to him. However, before a suitable opportunity had presented itself, the Kid had entered the saloon. On following, Roxterby had seen that there was a chance to kill two birds with one stone. He would avenge his employer and, at the same time, stop a discussion on the possibility of driving cattle to Kansas. There was a problem.

The supervisor recognized one of the seated quartet as the foreman of a ranch which had regularly brought cattle to the factory. Most likely the recognition would be mutual.

"All right," Roxterby said, deciding what to do. "Let's go and stop him."

Although the supervisor allowed the others to precede him through the batwing doors, he did not do it as a display of good manners. He had no intention of following them. Nor was fear of being recognized his only motive. From what he knew of the Kid, the intrusion would end with flying lead. Faced by odds of three to one, the Kid was almost certain to be killed. So whoever survived the attack would find themselves being hunted by his friends. Roxterby did not want men of Dusty Fog's caliber on his trail. By remaining outside, he would avoid being seen by the foreman. Nor could his companions identify him, for he had had another name when they had known him.

"I'll take him," Grift offered, slipping free his tomahawk and holding it behind his back.

Without realizing that they had been deserted by their companion, Abbot and Wolkonski followed Grift as he sauntered in a casual manner into the saloon. Once inside, they advanced in a loose V-formation which had Grift at its point.

The Kid glanced at the newcomers, but he decided that they were nothing more than customers in search of liquid refreshment. While the youngest looked like he was on the prod, that was only to be expected from one of his kind.

At another time, the Kid would have kept the trio under close—if not obvious—observation, especially Abbot. However, for once, he allowed himself to become so engrossed that he forgot to take the precaution. Returning his attention to the four cattlemen, he went on with his reasons for believing that large herds of cattle could be driven to the railroad in Kansas.

Bringing the tomahawk from behind his back, Grift threw it with the ease that told of long practice. Spinning through the air, its head sank into the edge of the counter's top about a foot to the right of the Kid.

"I say anybody's talks about driving cattle up to Kansas's *loco*," Grift announced as the Kid's words came to an abrupt end.

Despite having caused their victim to stop speaking, Grift felt that he ought to have achieved a more satisfactory result. Having had a tomahawk thrown so near to them, most men would have sprang away or shown some other sign of being startled. The black-dressed cowhand did not move a muscle. Somehow Grift formed the impression that it was not fright which was holding him immobile.

Although the four men who were sitting at the table swung their attention toward the intruders, they made no attempt to rise. Glancing at them, Grift hoped that they would not intervene. He could see no sign that they meant to do so. Probably they did not feel called upon to help the youngster deal with the interruption. Or they might be wanting to see if, after his big talk, he could stand up for himself. Whatever their reasons, Grift was grateful for their inactivity. That only left the bartender, and he was showing no inclination to interfere.

What Grift did not know was that the bartender had seen Roxterby's shadowy shape beyond the batwing doors. Although furious about the damage to the counter, he was waiting to discover what part the man outside was playing in the deal before stating his objections.

"And I backs ole *Nemenuh* all the way!" Abbot went on, oozing confidence and salty menace; or so he assumed.

"*Nemenuh*,[2] huh?" grunted the Kid and continued in the slow-tongued dialect of his maternal grandfather's people, the *Pehnane* Comanche, "Are you sure it shouldn't be 'Wormy'—or maybe 'Namae'enuh'?"[3]

Although Grift felt anger surging inside him at the

2. *Nemenuh* and *Pehnane* are translated for new readers in Appendix 2.
3. *Namae'enuh:* Put politely, "He-who-has-incestuous-intercourse."

words, it was swamped by a chilling realization of what he
had heard. His mother had been a *Waw'ai* squaw. Because
of their debased sexual habits—incest being commonly
practiced among them—and for other reasons, the *Waw'ai*
were rated very low by the other bands of the Comanche
nation. Their name, which meant "Wormy," was proof of
that. Not only had the baby-faced cowhand guessed with
which band Grift was associated, but he had spoken Comanche as if it was his native tongue.

Anybody who was so well conversant with *Nemenuh*
matters must have spent a considerable amount of time
among the People. Going by his youth, the black-dressed
cowhand might even have been raised by them.

Grift knew what *that* meant!

Maybe their "victim" would not be the easy mark they
had imagined!

Proof of that point was not long delayed!

On concluding his comment, the Kid reached out with
his right hand. Grasping the handle of the tomahawk, he
jerked its head upward and free. Then, reversing its direction, he flung the weapon with a deft ease which equaled
Grift's effort.

So swift and unexpected was the Kid's action, that it
took the men by surprise. Instead of returning the tomahawk in almost level flight, as it had been sent in his direction, he angled it downward. Letting out a yelp of alarm,
Grift made a rapid and long leap to the rear. It was fortunate that he did. With a solid "whunk!" the weapon buried
its cutting edge into the portion of the floor that had just
been vacated by his left foot.

For a moment, nobody moved or spoke. Then, as Grift
landed behind him, Abbot decided that the time had come
when he must take control of the affair.

Being inexperienced, but overconfident in his prowess as
a fighting man, the young hardcase felt that he had nothing
to fear. Maybe the black-dressed half-breed at the bar was
slick with a tomahawk, but that did not mean he was

equally good with a gun, especially with such a revolver as he was wearing. Effective as it might be as a man-stopper, the eight-inch-long barrel and four pounds one ounce weight of a Colt Dragoon did not permit real fast use. Certainly, in Abbot's opinion, one could not compare with the 1860 Army Colt in his own holster.

"That was pretty slick, 'breed," Abbot declared, taking two long strides forward and halting with the fingers of his right hand hovering over the Colt's butt. "How do you stack up with a white man's weapon?"

"Most times," the Kid answered quietly, yet exuding the latent and deadly menace of a cougar crouching to spring, "I don't even try."

"Could be you ain't got no chance but try *this* time," Abbot warned.

"Hold on there—!" began the tallest of the four ranch foremen, starting to rise.

"This's 'tween the 'breed 'n' me, mister!" Abbot spat out.

"You see it that way?" the foreman asked, directing the words to the young hardcase's companions.

"Boy gets something stuck in his craw," Wolkonski answered, "only thing to do is let him get it out."

"I've got no call for trouble with you," the Kid remarked, cold red-hazel eyes on Abbot's face. "So what's this all about?"

"You eating crow, 'breed?" Abbot mocked.

"Nope," answered the Kid. "I'm trying to stop you getting killed."

"Why thank you 'most to death!" the young hardcase sneered and reached downward. "Fill your hand!"

Which was just what the Kid proceeded to do.

Only not in the way that Abbot expected.

Flashing to the left, the Kid's right hand closed about the ivory hilt and plucked the knife from its sheath. His arm swung forward with considerable force, and at the appropriate moment he released his hold. Traveling horizontally and almost parallel to the floor, the weapon hissed through the air almost faster than the eye could follow.

Even as Abbot's revolver cleared leather, the clip point of the eleven and a half inch long, two and a half inch wide blade passed between his fourth and fifth left ribs. Such was the impetus of the throw that, backed by the weight and perfect balance forged in by James Black, the knife sank in to impale his heart. Stiffening as the sudden agony roared through him, he dropped the revolver and spun around with hands flying involuntarily toward the knife's hilt.

Once again, the speed of the Kid's reaction had taken his enemies by surprise. Nor was he content to leave it there. Grabbing the Winchester by the wrist of the butt with his left hand, he swung it from the top of the counter. His forefinger passed through the trigger guard, while the other three entered the ring of the loading lever. Coming over, his right hand caught the wooden foregrip that was a feature of the new type of weapon. One advantage the Henry and its immediate descendants had over most of their contemporaries was that they could be handled equally well with either hand. Down and up blurred the lever, cocking the action and sending a cartridge from the tubular magazine to the chamber in a single motion.

Nor was the precaution taken needlessly.

"Take him, Si!" Grift yelled, turning and springing toward the batwing doors.

Thinking that his companion was also starting to draw, Wolkonski grabbed for his gun. Just an instant too late, he realized that he was being deserted. There was no way out for him but to fight. So he continued with his draw and the Colt rose clear of its holster.

Noticing the speed with which Wolkonski was producing the revolver, the Kid knew that he could not hope to raise the rifle and use its sights. So he swiveled it around at waist level, realizing that he could not hope to shoot straight enough to ensure taking a wounded man capable of answering questions. Aiming by instinctive alignment, which was never conducive to extreme accuracy, he squeezed the trigger. With a crack, twenty-eight grains of du Pont black powder was detonated and thrust a flat-nosed .44 bullet from the barrel. It tore into the hardcase's breastbone, which snapped with an audible pop.

Even so, the Kid was only just in time. His lead arrived as the Colt was slanting its barrel toward him. Knocked backward by the impact, Wolkonski's revolver was deflected slightly. Not much, but enough. Fanning the Kid's cheek in passing, the bullet smashed a bottle behind the bar.

Throwing back their chairs, the four cattlemen rose with hands dipping toward their weapons. They watched Grift disappearing through the batwing doors, but were taking precautions in case he intended to return with friends.

"Let's separate!" Roxterby suggested, turning away as Grift erupted from the saloon. "I'll meet you at Ram Turtle's around midnight."

"You be there!" the hardcase replied and leapt forward. Without looking back, he raced toward the mouth of a dark alley across the street.

Springing along the sidewalk, Roxterby dived around the corner of the saloon. He fled as fast as his legs would carry him, swerving behind the rear of the next building. Then, stopping in the shadows, he listened for sounds of pursuit. Hearing nothing to suggest that he had been followed, he walked off at a more leisurely pace. Doing so, he realized, would be less likely to arouse suspicion than if he had kept running.

Being undecided as to what he should do next, the supervisor made his way toward the Belle Grande Hotel. He hoped that he would be able to discover de Froissart's whereabouts so that he could go and ask for advice. On approaching the open front door, he saw Viridian standing at the desk.

"Hey, boss!" Roxterby called. "I didn't expect to see you here."

Until he had heard Roxterby's voice, Viridian had been on the point of rushing upstairs to confront his wife and partner. Seeing Marlene's name in the register had explained several things which had been puzzling him. He now understood the reason for de Froissart's delay after he had knocked. It had been to let Marlene hide her discarded clothing under the bed and conceal herself in the wardrobe. He also knew why the Creole had come to the door holding the sword, despite having known who was outside.

There was no possibility that de Froissart had brought another woman and used Marlene's name as a means of obtaining accommodation for her. Marlene was too well known at the hotel for such a deception to have worked. What was more, the perfume Viridian had smelled in the room was his wife's favorite brand and she owned a gray Balmoral jacket which she frequently wore when traveling. Further proof was provided by the frank way in which the Creole had discussed the shootings in the afternoon. He knew that the listening woman could be trusted not to inform the marshal of what she had overheard.

Swiftly Viridian revised his intention of taking revenge upon his erring wife and partner. All too well he could see the objections to making the attempt immediately. If he returned to the room, de Froissart would suspect that he had learned their guilty secret no matter how calmly he behaved. In which case, everything would be in the Creole's favor. Viridian doubted whether de Froissart would rely upon the sword for he always carried a Remington Double Derringer and was equally skilled in its use. No longer would Viridian have the element of surprise, and with the hotel practically deserted there would be nobody to contradict whatever story the pair concocted to explain why he had been killed.

While bad-tempered and no coward, the burly man was

not hotheaded, impulsive, or rash. Having no desire to be killed, he thought fast and came up with a solution to his problem. One, moreover, which would prevent any suspicion from falling on him. Everything depended upon whether Roxterby would play the part assigned to him. Knowing the supervisor's avaricious nature, Viridian believed that he would.

"What brought you here?" Viridian demanded, turning and crossing the lobby. He waved Roxterby back as the supervisor was about to enter. "Wait outside."

"I came to see Mr. de Froissart," Roxterby explained when the burly man joined him on the sidewalk. "There's been some trouble."

"What happened?" Viridian demanded.

"I sent the fellers to stop the Ysabel Kid telling Caldicott from the Box Y and three more jaspers about trailing herds to Kansas."

"Did they do it?"

"No. He killed two of 'em and the other lit out of the saloon like his butt was burning."

"God damn it!" Viridian spat out. "Did Caldicott see you?"

"No," Roxterby replied, for the man in question had delivered herds to the factory. "When I saw he was there, I figured I'd best stay outside."

"Smart figuring," Viridian complimented, with only a trace of sarcasm in his voice.

"I thought you'd want it that way, boss," Roxterby answered, sounding relieved. "But this's getting dangerous. I wasn't counting on locking horns with the likes of Dusty Fog and the Ysabel Kid."

"Or me," the burly man admitted, before he could stop himself.

"We can't go on doing what you was wanting," Roxterby pointed out.

"Not now," Viridian conceded.

"Are we heading for Pilar?" the supervisor inquired hopefully.

"I am, but there's no reason why you shouldn't stay on here," Viridian replied, and seeing the alarm that came to the other man's face he went on in a placatory manner. "It's all right, Gus, I don't want you to go up against that OD Connected crowd. Do you reckon you can pick up some more men?"

"There'll likely be a few at Ram Turtle's place," Roxterby replied, referring to a saloon outside the city limits that was notorious as a rendezvous for bad characters of various kinds. "I could get 'em, but not if word's out that they'll be having fuss with Dusty—"

"That's not what I want them for," Viridian interrupted, glancing at the first floor of the hotel. "I've got something else in mind. There'll be five hundred dollars in it for you if you bring it off."

"*Five* hundred—!" Roxterby breathed.

"*And* there'll be a raise in pay for you back at the factory," Viridian continued.

"What do I have to do?"

"First off, don't let on to de Froissart that you've seen me. Then go along with him in what he wants doing all week. It won't be too dangerous—"

"Is *that* all?" Roxterby asked doubtfully, for he could not see the cause of his employer's promised generosity.

"Not quite," the burly man replied. "When de Froissart pulls out after the end of the Fair, I want him killed on the trail so that it looks like it was done in a holdup."

"But your missus'll be with him!" Roxterby protested. "Didn't you know she'd come—"

"I know," Viridian gritted. "And what I said still goes. See they don't get home alive and the five hundred's yours."

"You've got a deal, boss," Roxterby declared. "Start thinking of yourself as a widower."

6

CAPTAIN FOG WAS COLONEL
GOODNIGHT'S SEGUNDO

"I trust that you are fully recovered from that dastardly attack this afternoon, Captain Fog?" Governor Davis remarked, coming to a halt alongside the "short-growed, blond-haired kid" who had caused such a drastic alteration to the plans of the hide and tallow men.

Although the majority of Fort Worth's permanent and transient population were celebrating at the barbecue, the more important citizens and visitors had been invited to attend a ball in the Governor of Texas's honor at the home of the town's most wealthy businessman. Being General Ole Devil Hardin's segundo and, as such, representing a very powerful and influential faction in the State's affairs, Captain Dustine Edward Marsden Fog had naturally been included in the list of guests.

Dressed for the occasion in a well-cut black frock coat, frilly bosomed white silk shirt, black cravat fixed like a bow tie, brocade-decorated vest, and gray trousers, Dusty looked just a little more impressive than when wearing his usual working clothes, but not much. He had not left off his gun belt, nor changed his high-heeled boots, but they attracted neither attention nor comment. Most of the male guests, particularly those engaged in the cattle industry, had retained their weapons and traditional styles of foot-wear.

As Dusty's connections with Colonel Charles Goodnight were known among the ranchers who were present, he had been much in demand since his arrival. Circulating around the large dining room of Horatio Fitt's colonial-style mansion, he had been called upon repeatedly to tell what he knew of Goodnight's theories. He had also explained that his Uncle Charlie had traveled to Texarkana to act as escort for the Eastern cattle buyers, but would be back in time for the Convention. Finally, shortly before midnight, he found himself alone near the long table which held the refreshments and drinks supplied by his host.

Taking the first opportunity that had occurred since the small blond's arrival, Bartholemew Davis had come over to renew the brief acquaintance they had made earlier in the evening. Tall, thickset, jovial-looking, and dressed to the height of Eastern fashion, the Governor of Texas was first and foremost a politician. Although the people of the State had been disenfranchised for their support of the Confederacy in the War, so that he was appointed by Congress and not voted into office, he always tried to be on good terms with important and influential citizens. That was why he had sought out Dusty. Short in size and insignificant of appearance though he might be, the young blond was a person of consequence and must be treated accordingly.

"I'm well enough, sir," Dusty answered.

"I've been assured that Captain Dolman is a most efficient peace officer," the Governor commented. Knowing that few Texans had faith in the abilities of the State Police, he wanted to assure Dusty that everything possible was being done on his behalf. "And I'm confident that he'll bring the miscreant to justice."

"I hope he does," the small Texan drawled. "For Mr. Dover's sake, not mine."

"Of course," Davis agreed, although he had not given the dead rancher a single thought. Feeling a change of subject was called for, he went on, "I don't suppose there's any hope of General Hardin attending the Convention?"

"None, sir," Dusty replied. "Since his accident,[1] he hasn't been able to do any traveling."

"That was a tragedy," Davis declared, and sounded sincere. Which, as Dusty realized, meant little. He was a pretty good actor and used to simulating any emotion that he felt was required. "I'm sure that Colonel Goodnight would have appreciated his support."

"I can assure the Convention that Uncle Charlie's got it, sir," Dusty stated. "The General goes along with him that taking cattle to Kansas can get Texas back on her feet."

"Possibly," the Governor grunted in a noncommittal tone. "Possibly."

Realizing that he was approaching a *very* controversial subject, Davis's political training warned him to step warily. There were several of his supporters who would not wish to see Texas set back on the road to economic recovery. So he had no wish to be driven into making a definite statement; particularly to a man who had such close ties with the originator of the scheme to bring this about.

Looking around as he spoke, Davis sought for a way of avoiding further discussion. With a feeling of relief he saw a statuesque, elegantly gowned and jeweled, beautiful brunet woman coming toward him.

"Why, Marlene," the Governor greeted. "This is a pleasant surprise. I had no idea that you were here tonight."

Although Davis did not know it, such a comment was most unwelcome to Marlene Viridian at that moment.

After her husband had left the room, Marlene had emerged from the wardrobe. She and de Froissart had decided to refrain from any further lovemaking that night. While they had felt sure that Viridian did not suspect she had been present during his visit, they had realized that he would learn about her being in Fort Worth on his return to

1. Told in the "The Paint" episode of *The Fastest Gun in Texas*.

Pilar. So it was advisable that she should arrange an alibi ready for when he started to ask questions.

Having considered other alternatives, the Creole had suggested that—despite the lateness of the hour—Marlene should go to the barbecue. If she was lucky, she would meet one of the families she knew and be invited to spend the remainder of the visit with them. Certainly she ought to be able to make it appear that she had spent the whole evening away from the hotel.

Dressing sufficiently to allow her to return to her room at the other end of the passage, Marlene had changed hurriedly into more formal attire. Then she had made her way on foot to the barbecue. As she and de Froissart had not expected to require the coach that night, they had allowed its driver to go and visit some of his kinfolk in the town. That would be of use in the alibi, as the Negro would not be able to say at what time she had left the hotel. Viridian might be suspicious of her not retaining the services of the vehicle, but that could not be helped and might be explained convincingly.

On arriving at the barbecue ground, Marlene had heard about the Fitts' ball. Being acquainted with the businessman and his family, she had made her way to their mansion. Having seen the Governor as she entered, she had crossed the room to greet him. However, the last thing she wanted was for anybody to suggest that she had only just put in an appearance.

"I've been around for some time now, Governor," Marlene protested. "But you've been too busy to notice me."

"You should have come over as soon as you got here," Davis informed her, worried in case his preoccupation had been the cause of resentment.

"I didn't want to intrude," Marlene countered.

"Good lord, you wouldn't have," the Governor insisted. Rumor had it that Marlene wielded considerable influence with her husband and his partners, so he did not want her to feel that he had overlooked or snubbed her. Pilar Hide

& Tallow Company was a wealthy organization, which had frequently and generously contributed to what he termed his "campaign funds." There was a way, he decided, that he might make amends. If he knew the woman—and he believed that he did—she would be delighted to meet a man as socially prominent as his companion. "By the way, you do know Captain Fog, I suppose?"

"We've never met," Marlene admitted, looking around. "But I would certainly like to. I've heard so much about him. Is he here toni—?"

"This is Mrs. Viridian, *Captain Fog!*" Davis interrupted, laying emphasis on the last two words. He had acted with the smooth precision of a professional diplomat when it had become obvious that the woman had not connected the small Texan with the name he had mentioned. "Marlene, allow me to present Captain Dusty Fog."

Hearing the Governor's words and noticing the slight suggestion of alarm in his voice, Marlene swung her gaze from a man across the room who she had thought might be Dusty Fog. For a moment, she stared at the small Texan. If she was at all worried, or embarrassed, by her gaffe, she hid it very well.

For all that, knowing Davis would not be joking about his companion's identity, Marlene was puzzled. She wondered how such a diminutive youngster could have been involved in a fight with her husband and two hardcases, yet had emerged unmarked.

Glancing nervously at Dusty, the Governor sought for any suggestion that he had been offended by Marlene's behavior. Many a young man, having attained so much fame and responsibility, would have been and might have held it against the person who had made the disastrous introduction. Nothing showed on the blond's tanned face, so Davis concluded—not without a sensation of relief—that he had failed to notice the woman's reaction, or he had not understood what it had implied.

While Dusty had both observed and understood, he did

not let it worry him. He had long since grown accustomed to people registering surprise, sometimes even disbelief, on learning his identity. Studying Marlene in return, he formed conclusions about her character which were—if not complimentary—very close to being correct.

"My pleasure, ma'am," Dusty drawled, trying to remember where he had heard the name "Viridian."

"Charmed," Marlene responded, yet she was impressed despite her earlier feelings.

There must be, the woman told herself, much more to the small blond than met the eye. It could not be purely on account of his Civil War exploits that the Governor had displayed alarm when she had failed to recognize him. Any Texan—an ex-Confederate at that—who had such an effect upon Davis must either be important in contemporary affairs, or have connections with people who were. Perhaps Captain Fog might be worth cultivating. Manipulated correctly, after becoming infatuated by her charm, he could be useful in dissuading other ranchers from accepting Goodnight's suggestions.

"Is Austin with you?" Davis inquired, making conversation in the hope that the awkwardness caused by the introduction would be forgotten.

"No," Marlene replied. "He couldn't come."

"He's enjoying good health, I hope," the Governor went on.

"Yes," the woman answered, without thinking. Then, remembering what she ought to have said, she realized that she could no longer use the excuse which had been arranged. "He didn't feel up to traveling. He—sprained his wrist badly. A bull he was going to kill dropped its head. The poleax glanced off the boss of the horns and hit the wall."

Watching Marlene and listening to the explanation, Dusty sensed that she was lying. Unless he was mistaken, the reason she had given for her husband's absence had been invented on the spur of the moment. There had been a slight hesitation before she had mentioned his injury, as if she was trying to think up an acceptable story.

"Marlene's husband is a partner in the Pilar Hide & Tallow Company, Captain Fog," Davis elaborated, breaking in on the blond's thought-train. "Perhaps you know him?"

"No, sir," Dusty confessed, but did not mention that he had heard stories about Viridian's activities as a slaughter man. "I can't say that I do."

"Where do you sell your cattle, Captain?" Marlene inquired, feeling perturbed by his scrutiny. It was not the kind she would have expected from a small young man confronted by her sophisticated beauty, being more critical than openly admiring.

"At Brazoria, ma'am," Dusty replied.

"But you'll be trying to drive a herd to Kansas, I suppose?" Davis put in and immediately wished that he had kept quiet, for he was trespassing once more on dangerous ground.

"It's likely, sir," Dusty admitted.

"But surely your em—" Marlene began, but halted and revised her words before she could say "employer." *"You* don't believe that fool—"

"Captain Fog was Colonel Goodnight's segundo on the drive to Fort Sumner, Marlene," Davis interposed hurriedly, wishing to prevent the woman from making another embarrassing comment. Then he looked at Dusty. "Isn't that what they called you, Captain Fog?"

"I was called a whole lot worse at times," Dusty confessed with a grin. It departed as his gaze returned to Marlene. "Do you-all reckon it'd be foolish to try and reach Kansas with a herd, ma'am?"

"Good heavens!" the woman gasped, assuming an air of bewilderment that was almost successful. "How would *I* know about things like that?"

There was, if Dusty had read her character correctly, a good chance that she had definite and informed views on the matter. Before he could speak, however, he noticed something which gave him an added clue.

On the point of saying that Marlene was as shrewd in business matters as her husband, or his partners, Davis changed his mind. Going by her words and attitude, such a compliment would not endear its maker to her.

Watching the Governor open his mouth, but close it with the words unsaid, Dusty made an accurate guess at the reason. It helped to confirm his supposition that the woman's pretense of ignorance in the matter was very apparent, to the Governor as well as himself.

"I thought maybe that's how your husband and his partners feels about it, ma'am," Dusty remarked and continued with a comment which he felt sure would *not* be appreciated by Marlene. "I wouldn't expect a lady like you to know one way or the other."

"Of course I don't," Marlene gritted, and try as she might, she could not entirely conceal her annoyance at the condescending note in the young blond's voice. Making an effort, she went on in a milder tone, "My husband *never* discusses business in my presence."

"No, ma'am," Dusty drawled, driving home the spur even deeper. "I don't reckon he would at that."

Knowing something of Marlene's temper when crossed, Davis wondered if he should separate her and the small Texan. Despite Dusty's capability in other lines, including handling a mission which must have required considerable diplomacy,[2] Captain Fog appeared to be sadly lacking in tact and a poor judge of character. Or perhaps, filled with a sense of his own importance, he might have an overinflated opinion of masculine superiority upon a mere woman.

Whatever the blond's reasons, his attitude was liable to infuriate Marlene. It could easily bring about such an unpleasant scene that the Governor would find it necessary to intervene. His experience in such affairs was that, no mat-

2. Told in: *The Ysabel Kid.*

ter how good the intentions, the would-be mediator invariably incurred the enmity of one side or the other. So he looked around, searching for an excuse to take either Marlene or the young blond away.

For her part, the woman was struggling to keep control of her temper. She had always bitterly resented the way in which men automatically assumed that members of the opposite sex were incapable of understanding business matters. It was even worse when the condescension was emanating from such a small and insignificant—

Small?

Insignificant?

Suddenly Marlene felt as if a change had come over the blond. He seemed to have developed in height until he towered over her. While she realized that the transformation was only an illusion, she was equally aware of how it had been created. She was experiencing the full force of a very powerful personality.

Then another realization struck home at Marlene. The *big* blond's words had not been merely the tactless comment of a brash, inexperienced youngster who was trying to impress a beautiful woman with his worldliness. They were designed to goad her into incautiously displaying the extent of her knowledge. Or to gain information regarding the Pilar Hide & Tallow Company's feelings toward ranchers attempting to take cattle, which might otherwise have been brought to their factory, to the markets envisaged by Colonel Goodnight.

Until that moment, Marlene had continued to toy with the idea of exerting her charms upon the young Texan. Once he had grown infatuated by her, which she believed would be a foregone conclusion, she would be able to turn him against the idea of trying to drive a herd to the railroad. Possibly she could also persuade him to sign a contract with the Company.

Pleasing as the idea had been, particularly as it had offered the opportunity to achieve something where her husband had failed, Marlene decided to forget it. In view of her latest discoveries about the *big* young man, it would never work. Possibly he would gain more from the attempt than would be returned.

A sensation of panic bit at Marlene as she found the blond's gray eyes studying her. They seemed to be trying to probe into her and read her innermost thoughts.

Why had he acted in such a manner?

Did he suspect that her husband had led the attack upon him and guess what had motivated it?

Only by exercising her willpower considerably did Marlene fight down an inclination to turn and run away. While she succeeded, she also realized that she must get clear of the *big* Texan before he contrived to make her betray herself, or the Company.

Trying to act in a casual manner, as if bored by the conversation, Marlene swung her gaze around the room. People stood in groups, talking as they waited for the next dance. Not far away she saw her hostess engaged in conversation with two of the male guests. One was a rancher who had frequently sold cattle to the Company. The other was the young man she had believed to be Dusty Fog.

Studying the second of the guests, Marlene decided that he was by far the best-looking man in the room. Six feet three inches at least in height, not counting the addition of his high-heeled, fancy-stitched cowhand's boots, he had curly, golden blond hair and an almost classically handsome face. Clad in the same general manner as Dusty Fog, he showed off his clothes to a much better advantage. He had tremendously wide shoulders, which trimmed down to a lean waist and long, powerful legs. Ivory-handled Colt 1860 Army revolvers, of the finest blue "Best Citizen's Finish" offered by their manufacturers, rode the contoured holsters of his brown floral-patterned gun belt. Yet, despite its appearance, it was the functional rig of a man skilled in the use of his weapons.

That latter aspect interested Marlene, but not as much

as the blond giant's physical attributes. There was a man who might prove very useful. No more than Dusty Fog's age, he too carried himself with an air of easy assurance. It would be a pleasure to try to win him over. Alongside him, every other man she had known—even Harlow Dolman—seemed ordinary.

"Excuse me, Governor, Captain Fog," Marlene said, trying—and failing—to keep the dislike out of her voice as she uttered the last two words. "I must go and say 'hello' to Amanda Fitt."

While Marlene had been examining the blond giant, Davis had also been searching the room. Even as she addressed him, he had seen a solution to his problem.

"Of course," the Governor replied and, as the woman walked away, remarked to Dusty, "I wonder what's brought Marshal Grillman here." He indicated the open French window at the front end of the room. "Your man's with him."

Following the direction of the Governor's gaze, Dusty saw Marshal Grillman and the Ysabel Kid standing just outside on the porch. He guessed that they had come to see him and drew another conclusion from their attitudes. It was one which caused him to revise his plans. He had hoped to find out how the Governor regarded Goodnight's idea for rebuilding Texas's war-ruined economy, having been told to do so, if possible, by General Hardin. Clearly Davis did not wish to discuss the matter and he was showing signs of wanting to bring their meeting to an end.

"Likely they're wanting to talk to me," Dusty answered. "Excuse me, sir. I'll go and find out if they are."

"Certainly," Davis replied. "And I'd better start circulating."

"Marlene, darling," Mrs. Fitt greeted as the woman approached her group. "I'd no idea you were in Fort Worth."

"I only arrived this afternoon, but I felt sure that you wouldn't mind if I came along without being invited," Marlene replied, glancing at the big blond.

"Is Austin with you, dear?" Mrs. Fitt inquired, seeing at whom the brunet was looking.

"No," Marlene answered. "He couldn't come. He's bed-ridden with the grippe."

Almost as soon as the words had left the woman's mouth, she regretted them. Captain Fog was approaching and could have heard what she said. If he had, he might remark that she had made a different excuse to the Governor for her husband's absence.

7
HE'D FIT THE DESCRIPTION

For a moment, Marlene Viridian was worried. Then, as the small Texan continued to walk across the room, she decided that he had not heard her. Or if he had, he was content to mind his own business. Her eyes swung toward the rancher.

"Hello, Mr. Burton," Marlene said.

"Howdy, Mrs. Viridian," the cattleman answered, but he seemed to be ill at ease over meeting her. That could have been why he went on, "Do you know Mark Counter?"

"I haven't had that pleasure," Marlene confessed, turning on her most winning and gracious smile. Making a closer examination of the blond giant, she found no reason to revise her previous summation regarding his physical attributes. "Are you a rancher, Mr. Counter?"

"No, ma'am," Mark replied.

"Then you're not here for the Ranch Owners' Convention?" Marlene asked.

"Well, yes ma'am, I am," Mark contradicted. "I'll be speaking for my pappy's R Over C brand."

At that moment, the four-piece band started to play.

"Gracious me!" Marlene gushed, looking coyly at the big Texan. "I haven't had a dance all evening. Perhaps one of you gentlemen will take pity on me?"

Giving Burton no time to speak, or move, Marlene stepped in Mark's direction. Ignoring the cold glare darted at her by Mrs. Fitt, who had clearly been hoping that she would have the blond giant for her partner, Marlene accepted—almost grabbed—his arm and they went toward the center of the room. A slight frown came to her face as she watched Dusty Fog going through the French windows toward Marshal Grillman and the Ysabel Kid.

Wondering what had brought the two men to the mansion and if it was connected with the killings of the afternoon, Marlene became conscious of the powerful muscles in Mark's forearm. Clearly he was a man of considerable strength. Yet he moved lightly on his feet and without any suggestion of clumsiness. In all probability, he would be a very capable fighting man.

Glancing up at her escort, Marlene reached a decision. She would exercise all her charm upon him. If she could win him over, he might prove a very useful weapon and a more loyal ally than Harlow Dolman. Such a man, properly handled, could be invaluable in her future dealings with her husband. He might also be capable of dealing with Dusty Fog if the need arose.

"Howdy, Rupe, Lon," the small Texan drawled, not knowing that he was the subject of Marlene Viridian's thoughts. Having studied the two men since first seeing them, he had guessed that they were bringing bad, or disturbing, news. "What's the trouble?"

"You-all allowed he'd figure there'd been trouble, but I told you he wouldn't," the Ysabel Kid stated, eyeing the marshal as if he had proved a point instead of just the opposite. "I *knew* he'd reckon we'd come to join in all these high-toned doings and fancy foot-stompings."

"Is he like this all the time, Dusty?" Marshal Rupert Grillman asked, in tones redolent of mock resignation.

A tall, red-haired, angular man in his early thirties, the peace officer wore a town-dweller's suit, shirt, and tie, but sported a white Stetson, range boots, and a gun belt that carried an Army Colt in its fast-draw holster. There was an air of quiet competence about him that the law-abiding citizens of Fort Worth were finding most reassuring after the corruption and inefficiency of the State Police.

"Only when he's awake," the small Texan replied. "Which's never when there's any work to be done." Then he became more serious. "What's happened?"

"Trouble, like you figured," Grillman answered. "Let's take a walk in the garden so's we can talk in private." His eyes flickered at the Kid and he went on, "Company I'm keeping, I'd's soon not go anywhere's I'll be seen by folks who know me."

"That's not why he won't go inside," the Kid informed Dusty. "He don't want folks saying, 'Who-all's that old saddle-tramp with the Ysabel Kid?' And I'm not keen on going in, neither. Being seen with low-class folks like him wouldn't do me no good socially."

"Who taught you to say words like 'socially'?" the marshal challenged.

"I know a heap of other long 'n's as well," the Kid warned. "Happen we'd more time, I'd use 'em, not that *you'd* know what they mean."

"I don't mind Rupe standing here jawing about nothing," Dusty growled. "The good tax-paying citizens of Fort Worth hire and pay him, but *you're* working for the OD Connected and this's on our time."

"Somebody's trying to tell us something, Rupe," drawled the Kid, unabashed by the small Texan's cold-eyed scrutiny. "Let's get going."

Looking into the room, Dusty's eyes came to rest on Marlene and her partner as they danced by. If anybody had been watching, they might have noticed that the blond giant darted what might have been an inquiring glance at the small Texan and apparently received a quick, but negative, shake of the head in return.

If the byplay had meant anything, Dusty did not mention it as he walked away from the building with his visitors.

Finding a secluded part of the garden, he got straight down to business.

"What's this blasted varmint been up to *this* time, Rupe?" Dusty demanded.

"Me!" yelped the Kid, contriving to sound amazed and indignant, while looking as innocent as a pew filled with choirboys singing for the bishop.

"You," Dusty confirmed.

"Anybody'd reckon's I got into trouble's regular's Red Blaze,[1] when it ain't never but two-three times in any one week," the Kid protested. Then, dropping the levity, he told the small Texan about the trouble at the Post Oaks Saloon. He tried not to forget any of the details and concluded by saying, "I had to kill 'em both. There wasn't time for nothing fancy like trying to take 'em alive for questioning. Couldn't find hide nor hair of them other two, neither, what with having to wait until the law got around to coming 'n' asking what all the fuss was over."

"I mind the time when you wasn't so all-fired eager to wait around for the law," Grillman commented, thinking back to the days when the Ysabel family had been engaged in smuggling along the Rio Grande. "But I'm—"

"They was *better* days too," grunted the Kid. "I didn't have to wait—"

"Like I was going to say, when I got interrupted," the marshal went on. "But I'm right pleased there's been a change for the better."

"There's some's'd say it was for the *worser,"* the Kid sniffed. "If I hadn't waited—"

"Or that *any* change in you'd have to be for the *better,"* Grillman continued. "What do you reckon set 'em after him, Dusty?"

"Were they drunk, Lon?" the small Texan inquired.

"Not so's it showed," answered the Kid. "And I don't

---

1. Red Blaze: not in this book; Dusty's cousin and a member of the floating outfit, who has the reputation for becoming involved in fights.

recollect ever having crossed their trail to 've got 'em all riled up at me."

"Way you told it," Dusty said pensively, "they seemed tolerable set on stopping you talking about trailing herds to Kansas."

"That's how it sounded to me. Unless they was just feeling ornery and on the prod 'n' figured it'd be a good way to start trouble," the Kid replied and darted a defiant glance at the marshal. "Which, afore I gets asked, I don't believe neither. Maybe the young cuss'd've done it, but the other two would've been too slick for such foolishness. They wasn't yearling stock. Happen they'd just been on the prod, they'd've wanted somebody's'd've been a damned sight safer than me. Especially with the company I was keeping."

"Much's I hate to admit it, I'll go along with you on that, Lon," Grillman stated. "What do you make of it, Dusty?"

"Going by what Lon's just said," the small Texan replied, "it could be tied in with those three jaspers who tried to jump me."

"I thought you figured they were trying to rob you?" Grillman objected.

"That's how it looked at first," Dusty admitted. "But I wasn't too sure about it all along. I couldn't see why they would try to rob me, I didn't look like I'd be carrying anything worth stealing. On top of that, they hadn't robbed the rancher before they came after me. I'd seen one of them looking around the corner, then duck back like he didn't want to let me know he was there. They'd have had time to empty Dover's pockets before they came."

"Maybe they wanted to make sure you didn't get to the alley and see what they was doing," the Kid suggested.

"So why did all three of them come?" Dusty wanted to know. "One could have been robbing Dover while the other two 'tended to me."

"I only asked the question," the Kid protested. "I didn't aim to answer the son-of-a-bitching thing."

"Why thank you, 'most to death," Dusty said sarcastically. "I was even more sure that it wasn't just for robbery when I heard what the undertaker and doctor had told you, Rupe."

While laying out Dover's body, his wife having decided to let him be buried in Fort Worth's graveyard, the undertaker had noticed considerable discoloration on the abdomen and testicles. On being called to investigate, the doctor had confirmed that both areas were badly bruised. He had informed the marshal, who had passed on the news to Dusty.

"Them injuries had me worried," Grillman confessed. "He must've been unconscious, or so close as made no difference, when that bastard shot him."

"He sure aimed to kill him," the Kid went on. "Shot and missed once, then made damned sure it didn't happen again."

"And that was at a feller who couldn't've done anything to stop him," the marshal continued.

"But could have identified him," Dusty pointed out.

"So could you," the Kid reminded him.

"I could say what he looked like," Dusty corrected. "Maybe Dover could have put a name to him."

"What've you got in mind about this, Dusty?" Grillman demanded.

"Not a whole heap," the small Texan answered. "Just a few loose ends that're starting to tie together. I'd just been talking to Dover about trailing to Kansas and he seemed eager to have a whirl at it. And Kansas was the first thing mentioned when the feller who got away came up to me. Has the posse come back?"

"Nope," Grillman growled. "And I'm not expecting them to find anything, for all Dolman's big talk. We should've gone along, Lon."

"You're needed here in town, Rupe," Dusty said. "And, to be fair, Dolman had him a point when he said he'd got a track-reader who he'd worked with before and knew."

"So you reckon those fellers jumped you because you'd been telling Dover about trailing to the railroad, huh?" the marshal asked, reverting to the main subject of the conversation. "That means he must've told them you'd done it."

"But not *who* you was," the Kid went on, looking at the small Texan. "They'd never've come after *you* that ways had they known."

"That's for sure," Grillman conceded without hesitation. "So it looks like Dover knowed them fellers, or was stopped and asked about Kansas. Either's likely. Near on everybody in town's talking about it. Which do you reckon, Dusty?"

"Either's likely," Dusty agreed. "Which means that somebody doesn't want folks thinking it can be done and're set on stopping the notion that it can."

"But who the hell'd want to do *that?*" the marshal demanded. "If it can be done and Colonel Charlie's right about them wanting so much beef in the East, the money it'll bring in's going to set Texas back on her feet."

"There's some's wouldn't want to see that," the Kid warned. "Soft-shell bastard's hates us for fighting for the South. Carpetbaggers and scalawags[2] who're getting good pickings while folks don't have any money. What'd old Carpetbag Davis reckon about it, Dusty?"

"He won't commit himself one way or the other," the small Texan replied. "But I don't reckon he likes the notion. Once Texas gets back on her feet, we'll get back the franchise and he'll be out of office."

"So it could be him and the rest of his Reconstruction scum!" growled the marshal. "I can't think of anybody else."

"How about the hide and tallow men?" Dusty inquired.

"Hell, yes!" Grillman exclaimed. "If the ranchers can

2. A carpetbagger was a Northerner who had come to take advantage of Reconstruction to make financial gains and a scalawag was a Southerner who had supported the Union and now helped the carpetbaggers.

sell their cattle for a good price at the railroad, they sure as hell-and-a-half won't take what the factories're paying."

"I'm not saying there's anything in it," Dusty drawled. "But I was just now talking to Mrs. Viridian and she didn't sound any too taken by the notion of folks trailing herds to Kansas."

"Viridian?" the marshal repeated, frowning. "You mean her whose husband does all the killing for the Pilar Hide & Tallow Company?"

"Sure."

"Is her husband in town?"

"Nope. She allows he's stayed at home. Why?"

"Because," Grillman said soberly, "apart from the clothes, he'd fit the description of the feller's got away. I couldn't figure who that one put me in mind of when you first told me about him."

"Her husband, huh?" Dusty asked.

"The height, heft 'n' color of his hair're the same," Grillman confirmed. "I couldn't swear to the kind of boots he wears, but he totes an ivory-handled Remington New Model Police revolver in a cross-draw rig."

Dusty nodded his acceptance of the points made by the peace officer. While Grillman might not have paid any attention to Viridian's footwear, he was certain to have noticed how the man was armed and carried the weapon.

"Only," drawled the Kid, "happen the lady's telling the truth, her husband's not in town."

"That's what she said," Dusty agreed. "But she doesn't seem sure why he stayed at home. She told the Governor that he'd sprained his wrist, but reckoned he was in bed with the grippe when she was talking to Mrs. Fitt."

"Whooee!" the Kid shrieked. "If she was lying thataways, he could be in town right now."

"Or left after he'd killed Dover," Grillman went on, darting a look around the garden to make sure that they were not being observed.

"Or he's had nothing to do with it," Dusty drawled.

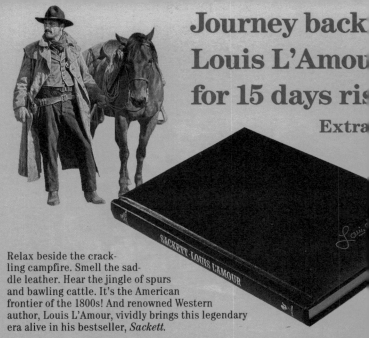

e Old West with
mpelling novel, *Sackett*,
e!

You may keep *Sackett* for only $4.95!*

*plus shipping and handling, and sales tax in NY and Canada.

Detach and mail this postpaid card to preview *Sackett* for 15 days risk-free and to claim your Free Gift!

RISK-FREE TRIAL CERTIFICATE
FREE GIFT!   FREE PREVIEW!

SAVE OVER HALF OFF!

☐ **YES.** Send my free Louis L'Amour Wall Calendar and my hardbound Collector's Edition of *Sackett* for a 15-day risk-free preview. If I keep it, I'll honor your invoice for only $4.95—a SAVINGS OF OVER HALF OFF the current low regular rate of $11.95—plus shipping and handling, and sales tax in NY and Canada. Then I'll continue receiving additional selections about once a month at the regular rate on the same 15-day risk-free trial basis. There's no minimum number of books I must buy, and I may cancel at any time. The Calendar is mine to keep no matter what I decide.

IL6   41400

Name _____ (please print)

Address _____ Apt. ____

City _____ State _____ Zip ____

SEND NO MONEY NOW

Prices subject to change. Orders subject to approval. Prices shown are U.S. prices.

In Addition to the Free Louis L'Amour Calendar

. . . your risk-free preview volume of *Sackett* will introduce you to these outstanding qualities of the bookbinder's art—

- Each volume is bound in rich, rugged sierra-brown simulated leather.
- The bindings are sewn, not just glued, to last a lifetime. And the pages are printed on high-quality paper that is acid-free and will not yellow with age.
- The title and Louis L'Amour's signature are golden embossed on the spine and front cover of each volume.

SAVE OVER HALF OFF!

BUSINESS REPLY MAIL

FIRST CLASS MAIL   PERMIT NO. 2154   HICKSVILLE, NY

POSTAGE WILL BE PAID BY ADDRESSEE

The Louis L'Amour Collection
Bantam Doubleday Dell Direct, Inc.
PO Box 956
Hicksville NY 11802-9829

NO POSTAGE
NECESSARY
IF MAILED
IN THE
UNITED STATES

◀ Detach
and
mail
this
postpa
card
to
get
The
Louis
L'Amou
Calend
absolu
FREE!

"There could be other reasons why she didn't tell the same story about him."

"Sure," Grillman admitted. "But—"

"But there'd be a few things explained if it was Viridian," Dusty finished for the marshal. "He's a hide and tallow man and likely wouldn't want Uncle Charlie's notion to come off. So he could've come here to try and make sure that it didn't. Maybe Dover used to sell cattle to their factory, which'd explain how Viridian knew him—and why Dover was killed. Figuring a deputy'd been shot, Viridian wouldn't want anybody around who could put a name to him. He showed that when he gunned down his own man."

"You'd seen him up close and could recognize him again," the Kid pointed out, having forgotten that he had already raised that point.

"But I couldn't *name* him," Dusty repeated. "That's where the difference lies. And you didn't give him the chance to make sure of me."

"Thing being," Grillman said, "where's he at now?"

"In town somewheres," the Kid suggested. "Or headed for Pilar's fast's his hoss can carry him."

"I don't reckon he'd chance staying in town," Grillman declared. "Not with his missus telling folks he's back at home with whatever ails him. I could telegraph the constable at Pilar and ask if he is there, but I'll likely get told he is, no matter what's the truth of it. The town belongs to the Company."

"There's another way of checking," the Kid remarked, looking hopeful as he saw an opportunity of leaving Fort Worth before he could be drawn into some kind of social activity that might entail dressing formally. "I could be there 'n' back in two-three days, riding relay."

"Happen Viridian pulled out straight after the killing, he'd beat you to Pilar," Grillman objected. "And he'll likely not be traveling slowly. Not even *you* and that blasted Nigger hoss of your'n could get there ahead of him."

"I wouldn't be that far behind," the Kid grunted.

"Likely," Grillman conceded. "But he'd be there already and, happen he recognized you—which he'd be likely to do —I don't reckon he show his good ole Northern hospitality."

"You didn't see the feller who stayed outside the Post Oaks, Lon?" Dusty put in.

"Not clear enough to go and say, 'I know you, come 'n' have a drink,'" the Kid replied. "He kept back in the shadows. Do you reckon it was him?"

"It could be," Dusty drawled. "If it was, that'd be another reason for having those yahoos jump you. He wouldn't be holding too many friendly feelings for you after what happened."

"So he could still be around town," Grillman growled.

"Or somewhere close by," Dusty answered. "I don't see a feller that mean giving up easily. So he might be staying on, ready to keep stirring up more trouble."

"If he is," the Kid commented, "he's likely needing some more hired help. What say we drift on over and say 'howdy' to good ole Ram Turtle, Rupe?"

"I'd say that, for once in your life, you'd had a right smart notion, Lon," the marshal declared.

"Let me go and say 'Good night' to the Fitts," Dusty requested, knowing the nature of Ram Turtle's establishment and also that Grillman had no official standing there. "And I'll come along."

"Ram'll sure be honored," grinned the Kid, eyeing Dusty's attire. "With you-all dressed so fancy, he'll figure you've done it for him."

8

YOUR BADGE DON'T
MEAN A THING

Although midnight had passed, lights were blazing and considerable noise suggested that people were up and about in the Snapping Turtle Saloon. Halting their mounts at the edge of the clearing in which Ram Turtle's establishment was situated, Dusty Fog, the Ysabel Kid, and Marshal Rupert Grillman studied the two main buildings and the surroundings. A number of horses lined the hitching rail and more were moving around in the corral at the rear. Not far from the enclosure was a three-holer backhouse, and a light which showed from beneath one of the doors suggested that the cubicle was occupied.

"There's a fair crowd still around," the Kid remarked, lounging comfortably on his magnificent white stallion's low-horned, double-girthed Texas saddle. The animal looked almost wild, yet remained attentive to its rider's slightest indication of what would be required from it next. "No decent, law-abiding folks'd be a-whooping 'n' carousing this late."

"You expected maybe to find *law-abiding* folks *here?*" Grillman demanded.

Sitting on a big bay gelding, the marshal was dressed in what he regarded as suitable attire for visiting Ram Turtle's saloon. Before leaving Fort Worth and setting off on the

two-mile ride, he had visited his office to collect certain
items which he had believed might be required. One of
them was the long Confederate States' Cavalry cloak-coat
which he had donned.

"*I* was here a couple of times with pappy," the Kid
pointed out.

"So what does that prove?" the marshal challenged.

Before the Kid could comment, the batwing doors which
gave access to the main barroom were thrown open. A tall,
well-built young man lurched out, moving with the gait of
one who had taken a drink or two too many. Dressed in
dandified range clothes, he had a revolver with a set of
fancy, silver-inlaid Tiffany grips in an unusual type of holster. Stalking to where a fine-looking chestnut gelding was
standing, he fumbled with its reins and, cursing audibly,
managed to unfasten them from the hitching rail. He almost threw himself into the finely carved, dinner-plate
horned Mexican saddle and snatched at the animal's
mouth to make it turn. Then he used his spurs and set it
into motion. From his attitude, he was riled about something and wished to leave the vicinity as quickly as possible.

Dusty's party had halted amongst the trees while they
were examining the clearing. Although they had not taken
any great pains to conceal themselves, the young man
dashed by without showing any indication of knowing that
they were there.

"Know him, Dusty?" Grillman inquired, throwing a dis-
gusted look after the departing rider.

"Can't say I do," the small Texan replied.

"It's Garvin Fitt," the marshal drawled.

"Way you said that," drawled the Kid, "I'd bet you don't
care a whole heap for him."

"He drinks too much and has too much money,"
Grillman answered. "On top of that, he allows he's *eighteen*
hands high, with gravel in his guts, spit in his eyes, and can
do most anything he likes any old time."

"Man like that could get his-self to be a byword and a

hissing amongst decent folks," the Kid declared, raising his eyes piously to the sky as if afraid that Fitt's bad example might rub off on him.

"He's spoiled rotten by his folks and they think he can't do no wrong," Grillman growled. "He'd've been in scrapes a couple of times if it hadn't been for Harlow Dolman, who's a good friend of the family. Young Fitt even totes his Colt in one of them 'clamshell' holsters and allows he's a regular snake at pulling it. Not that he's tried to prove it— yet. Time's fast coming, 'less I miss my guess, when somebody'll have to pick up his toes."[1]

"Time's not standing still *here*," the Kid pointed out and nudged the stallion with his heels.

Directing a look which bounced off the Kid's back, Grillman allowed his horse to follow the big white. At Dusty's heel signal, his mount went along with the other two.

The seventeen hand paint stallion between the small Texan's legs was a hint of his true potential. Large, without being clumsy, and powerful, only an exceptional rider could control it. In fact, it had been responsible for the accident which had crippled General Hardin. Having broken and trained it after his uncle's mishap, Dusty showed that he was clearly in command. Yet his dominance had not been obtained by such cruel methods that the animal was left without will or spirit.

Nobody challenged the trio as they approached the saloon. Dismounting, Dusty and the marshal tossed their reins over the hitching rail but did not bother to fasten them. The Kid did not even go that far in securing his mount. Knowing that the white would remain where he left it, he knotted the reins loosely to the saddle horn. Reaching, he drew the Winchester rearward from its boot on the

---

1. Pick up his toes: a roping term, meaning to catch a horse or a steer by its forelegs causing it to fall heavily. Used as a means of punishing a recalcitrant animal.

left of the saddle. While he was doing that, Dusty removed
his jacket and draped it across the seat of the paint's rig.
However, the marshal did not take off the cloak-coat.
Rather, he made sure that it hung in such a way that it
concealed his arms, which were not inside its sleeves.

"Let's go say 'howdy' to good ole Ram," Grillman suggested.

"Not me," drawled the Kid, overlooking that the visit
had been his idea in the first place. "I'd as soon kiss a
skunk, or maybe sooner."

"We don't have one," Dusty pointed out. "Or I'd expect
you to do it."

"*You* would," sniffed the Kid.

Crossing the porch, the three men paused and looked
over the batwing doors. Experienced in such matters, they
knew better than to walk from darkness into a lighted
room before their eyes had become accustomed to the
change. That particularly applied when the room was in
Ram Turtle's saloon. So they used the time to study what
lay before them.

The big barroom was well filled and busy. There were a
few cowhands, some obvious town dwellers, but the majority of the customers were hard-eyed, gun-hung men in a
variety of dress styles. All had one thing in common, a
wolf-cautious alertness and vigilance. The saloon's staff
comprised of girls in gay, short frocks, a few professional
gamblers, burly bouncers, and a trio of equally large bartenders.

"Any sign of him?" Grillman inquired.

"Not's I can see," the Kid replied, having been looking
for *Nemenuh* Grift. "But he could be upstairs, if he did
come here."

"Best go in anyways," Dusty declared. "We're making
some of 'em nervous standing out here."

Suspicious eyes swung toward the door, or continued to
stare at it, as the Kid, Grillman, and Dusty entered. They

formed a line, with the marshal as its center, and started to walk toward the bar.

Rising from his seat at a table on a dais in the left rear corner of the big room, a place which allowed an unrestricted view of the bar and floor, Ram Turtle waddled down the steps. At his signal, the two biggest of the bouncers advanced and fell in slightly to his rear. Dressed in the style of a Mississippi riverboat gambler, Turtle had the face and moustache of a Bavarian innkeeper. Any joviality, however, was purely on the surface. Underneath, he was hard, ruthless, and completely devoid of moral scruples. Certainly there was nothing amiable about him as he came to a halt before the newcomers.

"Fort Worth ends a mile and a half back," Turtle declared, scowling at Grillman.

"I'd say a mite further than that," the marshal answered, keeping his hands out of sight beneath the cloak-coat.

"Your badge don't meant a thing outside the city limits," Turtle warned, glancing at Dusty and then subjecting the Kid to a longer scrutiny.

Standing with the Winchester trailing negligently in his right hand, the Indian-dark youngster met the saloonkeeper's gaze. He wondered if Turtle would identify him as he had not been wearing all black cowhand-style clothes on his previous visits.

While Turtle felt that he ought to know the Kid, he failed to come up with the right name. Then his eyes returned to Dusty and a slight frown came to his face. Shrewd judge of character, he sensed that the small blond was far from the least dangerous of the new arrivals.

"Are you saying I'm not welcome?" Grillman challenged, breaking in on the saloonkeeper's thoughts.

"That depends why you're here," Turtle answered, reverting his attention to the peace officer. "If Horry Fitt sent you after young Garvin, he's already pulled out."

"He didn't send me," the marshal declared.

Leaving his companions to do any talking that might be

necessary, the Kid scanned the room once more. He had
no greater luck in locating *Nemenuh* Grift, but noticed a
lantern's glow as somebody passed the left-hand wall's rear
window. He could not see the person, but guessed it was a
man returning from the backhouse. Although he had made
a thorough scrutiny of the crowd, the Kid could hardly be
blamed for failing to realize that he had seen the fourth of
the men who had come after him at the Post Oaks Saloon.

Standing at the bar, waiting for Grift to return from the
backhouse so that they could resume their discussion on
Viridian's requirements, Gus Roxterby had looked over his
shoulder when the trio made their appearance. He had
recognized the Kid immediately, but gambled upon not
being identified in his turn. To have turned and tried to
leave would have drawn unwanted attention his way. So he
had swung his head to the front and remained at the
counter. There was, he had concluded, no way in which he
could warn Grift. All he could do was hope that the other
should see the danger while coming from the backhouse
and stay out of the barroom.

"Ain't nobody but the State Police got jurisdiction in
here," Turtle was saying when, having hung the lantern on
the hook provided for that purpose, Grift opened the door.
"So, happen you're thinking of trying to arrest anybody,
forget—"

Even if the situation had been rehearsed for days, Grift's
entrance could not have been timed more perfectly. Turtle
was delivering an ultimatum and taking a stand from which
he could only retreat by losing face with his customers.

Noticing the way in which everybody was staring toward
the center of the room, Grift followed their example. His
eyes met those of the Ysabel Kid and he knew that the
recognition was mutual.

"Namae'enuh!" the Kid growled and lunged forward.

Shock showed on Grift's lean face and he began to with-
draw hurriedly from the room.

Turtle did not know who had come in, but realized that it

must be the person for whom his unwelcome visitors were looking. So there was, in view of his statement—which had mainly been made with the intention of impressing his customers—only one way in which he could act.

"Stop him!" the saloonkeeper snarled, sending the words over his shoulder to the pair of hardcases who were standing on either side and slightly to his rear.

Instantly, the bouncer who was confronting the Kid made a move as if intending to obey. Less observant than his employer, the second hardcase turned his eyes from Dusty to see if any help would be needed. In various other parts of the big room, further members of the staff showed signs to suggest that they too intended to lend a hand. A dealer at the faro table on the right side of the room thrust back his chair, started to rise, and reached for his gun; which caused the players in his game to hurl themselves hurriedly out of the possible line of fire. The largest of the bartenders moved along toward the sawed-off shotgun which was kept on a shelf under the counter. Over by the door, which Grift was closing as he departed, yet another gambler also began to leave his seat.

Instead of displaying perturbation, or alarm, at being menaced by the huge bouncer, the Kid acted with the speed—if not the full lethal capability—of a *Pehnane* Dog Soldier. Pivoting slightly from the hips, while continuing his advance, he swung the rifle in his right hand back, then around, up, and down. The eight and a half pound weapon slashed its barrel against the side of the man's head and sent him sprawling away to fall as if he had been poleaxed. Almost before he had landed on the floor, the Kid was striding by and making for the door. There were other enemies, the Indian-dark youngster realized, who might try to dispute his right to go after Grift.

Seeing the Kid starting to launch the attack, the second bouncer grabbed at his holstered revolver. He did not believe that the small blond would be a considerable factor in the game and was sure that his boss could deal with the Fort Worth peace officer.

Confident that his employees were capable of upholding his boast—and that Captain Harlow Dolman had been sufficiently well bribed to prevent any legal repercussions—Turtle glared into Grillman's eyes. Trying to hold the peace officer's gaze, he began to raise his right hand. His right elbow was moving toward his side, ready to press and operate the switch on the spring-loaded holster which would deliver a Remington Double Derringer into his palm.

Knowing that the best plan in such a situation was to handle things in a spectacular manner, Dusty acted accordingly. Darting forward, he bent and wrapped his arms around the bouncer's legs just above the knees. Giving a sudden, inward jerk, he snapped the legs together and, in doing so, destroyed the man's equilibrium. Then, exerting all his strength, Dusty straightened up. Raising the man from the floor, the small Texan thrust him backward and let go. Thrown through the air for a short distance, the bouncer lit down flat-footed. There were, however, others who would require Dusty's attention.

At the same moment that Dusty started to tackle the bouncer, Grillman prepared to deal with the threat to his own life. He knew all about the special holster attached to Turtle's wrist and was ready to counter it. Bringing his right hand from beneath the cloak-coat, he showed that it held the sawed-off shotgun which had been hanging suspended from a carbine sling.[2] Also appearing from beneath the garment, his left hand crossed to take hold of the weapon's foregrip. Behind Grillman, by the batwing doors, a man reached for his revolver.

Although the gambler near the left side's door had acted instinctively, he rapidly revised his decision. No longer did the Kid look babyishly innocent. Instead, his face had taken on the cold-eyed, savage aspect of a Comanche

2. A description of a carbine sling and its use is given in: *Go Back to Hell*.

tehnap[3] who was riding the war trail and hoping to count coup on the hated white-eye brother. Realizing that he might come into that category and noticing how the youngster now held the rifle in both hands, ready to use as a firearm rather than a club, the gambler sank back into his chair and exposed his open palms in a prominent manner. There were, he concluded as he glanced about him, colleagues better placed to deal with the Indian-dark Texan.

As always under such conditions, Dusty's mind was working with lightning speed and analyzing everything he saw. Taking note of the bartender's and faro dealer's actions, he was working out the best means by which he might prevent his amigo from being shot.

First and foremost, Dusty decided, the bouncer must be taken into consideration. Jolted off balance by the unexpected throw and landing, he was far from being incapacitated. Given an opportunity, even a brief one, he would regain control of his movements and be able to add to the danger.

With that in mind, Dusty followed the staggering man and acted before he had a chance to protect himself. Halting with his weight on his right foot, the small Texan tilted his torso to the right and bent his left knee. Keeping the lower part of the raised leg parallel to the floor, he rotated his hips sharply so that he swung his foot around. Curling forward, the toe of his boot drove into the bouncer's ribs.

Such was the force with which Dusty delivered the *mawashigeri,* outside roundhouse, kick—one of the *karate* and *jujitsu* tricks which he had learned from General Hardin's Japanese valet, Tommy Okasi—that the hefty bouncer was sent staggering. Colliding with a table, he fell across it and it collapsed under his weight. Yells of alarm and annoyance rose from the three men and two women who were using the table. Trying to avoid being pinned

3. Tehnap: an experienced and very capable warrior.

under it, they shoved back their chairs. They were too late
and all went sprawling to the floor.

With the bouncer removed, Dusty looked about him.
Already the bartender was starting to bring the shotgun
over the top of the counter and cocking its hammers. Acting no less swiftly, the faro dealer's right hand was snaking
a revolver from its holster. Each was making the Kid the
object of his attentions.

Concentrating at holding the marshal's eyes on his own,
for he was confident that his men could take care of the
two young Texans, Turtle made ready to arm himself. Then
his ears were assailed by several sounds which suggested
that things might not be going as he would have desired.
Most important of them was an ominous double click from
ahead, but below his line of vision; and certain significant
words uttered by the peace officer.

"You've got a big belly, Ram. And this scatter's got
mighty light triggers. Happen I was asked, I'd say you was
close to getting killed."

Lowering his eyes involuntarily, the saloonkeeper took
in the sight of the wicked-looking weapon. Then his gaze
lifted to where the man behind Grillman was starting to
raise a revolver.

Bringing his foot to the floor, Dusty sent his hands flashing inward to enfold the butts of the Army Colts. Three
quarters of a second later, they had cleared their respective
holsters' lips. Almost of their own volition, it seemed,
the seven-and-a-half-inch-long "Civilian Model" barrels[4]
turned at waist level toward the greater peril to the Kid.
Flame belched from each muzzle, but the two detonations
merged into a single sound.

Realizing that the shotgun in the bartender's hands was
likely to be more dangerous than the dealer's revolver,
Dusty sent the bullets in that direction. Flying the fifty or

4. The standard model, for sale to the military, had an eight-inch-long
barrel.

so feet which separated him from his intended target, the lead ripped into the bartender's neck and temple. Pain and the impact caused him to reel. Tilting upward, the shotgun was discharged without conscious thought on its user's part and eighteen buckshot balls peppered holes in the ceiling. Letting go of his weapon as he collided with the wall, the stricken man disappeared after it behind the counter.

Satisfied that his companions would protect him from the other occupants of the room, the Kid prepared to leave. Standing against the wall, he transferred his left hand to the handle of the door. Jerking it open, he scowled with disapproval at the hanging lantern which was for use by anybody who wished to visit the backhouse. While it might be an advantage in that respect, it threw a pool of light through which the Kid would have to pass. Not a pleasing thought, with an enemy waiting in the darkness.

Letting out a low grunt, the Kid catapulted himself forward. Muzzle blast flared redly from the front of the saloon, merging with shots from inside the building, and lead screamed above the Kid's diving figure. He landed in the darkness on his stomach and hoped that his black clothing would help to hide him. They did, to a certain extent. Grift's revolver spat again, to miss.

But not by much!

Dirt erupted as the bullet struck the ground, spraying fragments into the Kid's face. Letting go of the rifle, he grabbed at his stinging eyes in a desperate attempt to clear them. Loud to his ears came the sound of a revolver's mechanism being brought to full cock.

Swiveling the instant he saw that his shots had taken effect, Dusty flung his right-hand Colt to shoulder height and arm's length. With his revolver out, the faro dealer forgot his intention of throwing down on the Kid. Instead, he started to turn the barrel in Dusty's direction. Both weapons spoke at the same instant, but the small Texan was the better shot. Feeling the wind of the close-passing bullet, Dusty saw the man jerk as if struck by an invisible hammer. The .44 bullet had taken him in the right shoulder, but that proved to be sufficient. Knocked from his feet, he fell with the revolver slipping from a suddenly inoperative set of fingers.

With the thunder of Dusty's shots ringing in his ears, warning him that things were not going as was desirable, Turtle reached a decision. The man behind the marshal was getting ready to shoot, but the saloonkeeper no longer believed that it was such a good idea. Grillman held a cocked shotgun, with his right forefinger already tight on the triggers. No matter where the man's bullet hit him, he would complete the pressure and—as he had said—Turtle's stomach made a very large target. If the man fired, Grillman would die—but so would the saloonkeeper.

"No!" Turtle yelled, hating to have to say the words despite knowing that his only other choice was to get killed. "Don't do it!"

"I don't know if you're bluffing or not, Ram," the marshal drawled, without offering to look behind him. "But you've given good advice. There's only one thing'd make it better. See to it that nobody else throws lead. Because the next but one'll come out of *my* scatter—and you know who'll be the target."

"All right!" Turtle growled, conceding defeat and raising his voice. "Don't nobody make a move."

Still trying to clear his eyes, the Kid let out a shrill whistle. Trying to line his revolver on the vague shape, Grift heard an explosive snort and the sound of hooves. Turning his head, he saw a huge white stallion rushing at him. Spitting a curse, he began to swing his weapon round. Forward thrust the horse's neck and its teeth clamped hold of his wrist. With a savage jerk, it flung the man from his feet. Landing hard, Grift rolled. He looked up, to find the stallion looming above him. The shrill, wicked scream of an enraged *manadero*[5] rang out. Then ironshod hooves

5. Manadero: master stallion of a band of wild horses.

slashed down. Grift screeched once, the sound being followed by a sickening thud and another as the horse
stamped upon him.

Shaking his head, the Kid rose. While his eyes were still
stinging and sore, he could see through them. Gathering
up his rifle, he went to calm his stallion as it continued to
assault its victim. While grateful to the horse for saving
him, the Kid knew that he would not be given any answers
by *Nemenhuh* Grift.

9
I DON'T WANT ANY TROUBLE

"Have you wondered if perhaps Goo—Colonel Goodnight and his friends might have an ulterior motive for persuading other ranchers to try and reach Kansas with their herds?" Marlene Viridian inquired, sitting on the decorative stone wall of the porch and looking up at the blond giant.

After finishing the dance with Mark Counter, Marlene had continued with her plan to cultivate his acquaintance. Disregarding her hostess's thinly-veiled and obvious disapproval, she had remained in his company and contrived to carry on being his partner. She had made herself very pleasant, without openly flirting, and believed she had suggested to him that she was willing to go farther at a more suitable time.

While dancing and talking, Marlene had formed an assessment that was much in the big Texan's favor. He drank sparingly, which might prove a mixed blessing in view of what she had planned for him, and he struck her as being intelligent. Certainly he was anything but a naïve, fairly wealthy, small-town bumpkin. Nor would he, unfortunately, be an easily controlled tool. However, she was even more certain that he would be suitable for her needs.

With her decision reached, Marlene had suggested that

they should step outside for a breath of fresh air. She had done so in such a way that she implied there might be more than that in store for him. Going through the open set of French windows at the right side of the dining room, she had moved along the porch into the shadows. Halting where they could not be seen by the other people attending the ball, she had sat on the wall and steered the conversation to the topic which was uppermost in practically everybody's thoughts in Fort Worth.

"What would that be?" Mark inquired, remaining on his feet and at a decorous distance.

"If enough of them try it, there will be a shortage of cattle at the hide and tallow factories," Marlene explained, trying to read some evidence in his face of how he was taking the words. He seemed interested, so she continued, "The prices will go up and that would be to the advantage of anybody who *hasn't* taken herds to the railroad."

"Do you reckon that's what Goodnight has in mind?" the blond giant growled, and to the woman's delight he sounded indignant.

"It's possible," Marlene stated. "Do you believe that *anybody* could drive a herd all that way?"

Before Mark could make a reply, a shadow fell in the lighted area beyond the French windows. Glancing by the big Texan, Marlene frowned as she recognized the person who was emerging from the dining room. Turning his head, Mark also looked. What he saw caused him to swing around slowly and face the newcomer. While he did not know the young man, or connect him with the Fitt family, Mark drew some fairly accurate—and a few erroneous—conclusions regarding him. One was that it might be advisable to keep him under observation.

Some people might have mistaken Garvin Fitt for a cowhand, but the blond giant would not be one of them. He knew that the young man had never worked with cattle and suspected that he had rarely indulged in labor of any kind, but was merely dressed—overdressed in fact—to look as if

he had. However, the fancy-handled revolver in the split-
fronted holster hung right for a fast draw. The rig itself was
unusual. Apart from the drop of the holster being longer
and having more of the weapon exposed, it resembled one
used by Mark's cousin, Solly Cole.[1] He wondered what, if
any, advantage the differences offered.

However, the blond giant gave only a little thought to
that aspect. His main interest was directed at Fitt. The
flushed cheeks, lurching gait, and general attitude displayed by the newcomer acted like a warning beacon to
Mark. There, unless he read the signs wrongly, stood a
potential hardcase who was on the prod and looking for
trouble.

In the latter summation, Mark was doing Fitt an injus-
tice. While normally an arrogant bully and not averse to
making trouble, it was worry that was responsible for his
attitude. After losing heavily in a poker game at the Snapping Turtle, despite knowing that his father had sworn not
to help him pay off any more of his gambling debts, the
young man had signed an IOU for five hundred dollars.
There was certain to be a very unpleasant scene when Fitt
Senior heard about his son's latest losses, but that was less
disturbing than the thought of what Ram Turtle would do
if the money was not forthcoming.

On his return home, Fitt had hoped to meet Harlow
Dolman among the guests at the ball. Failing to do so, but
wishing to avoid having to explain his absence to his par-
ents, he had passed quickly through the dining room and
on to the porch. Finding that it was occupied, he looked at
the man and the woman.

Identifying Marlene, Fitt saw a glimmer of hope that he
might yet evade the consequences of his foolishness. On a
previous visit, she had been fairly attentive to him. Being
vain and used to having his ego fed by the girls in the

1. More details of Solly Cole's gun-rig are given in: *Calamity Spells Trouble*.

saloons he frequented, he had believed that she had been infatuated by his manly charm and virility. In which case, she might be persuaded to make him a "loan" of enough money to pay off Turtle. Or, failing that, she could exert her influence and win Dolman's support.

First, however, Fitt would need to get Marlene alone so that he could set about inducing the necessary receptive mood. To do that, he would have to separate her from the big, blond dandy. Being in a frame of mind where he believed himself to be invincible, Fitt decided that it would present little or no difficulty.

"Hello there, Marlene," the young man said, swaggering forward. "Where's good old Austin, back at home having fun killing all the cattle?"

"He's at home, but ill with the grippe," the woman answered, and her voice held little welcome or encouragement. "It's growing chilly out here, Mark. Shall we go back inside?"

"How about having the next dance with me, Marlene?" Fitt suggested, making the words sound like a command, without giving the giant Texan time to speak.

"I'm afraid not," Marlene replied, standing up.

"Why not?" Fitt demanded, darting a more searching glance at the big blond and deciding that he was not yet twenty years of age. That confirmed Fitt's belief that he could easily scare or drive off his rival.

"I'm tired," Marlene stated, throwing an overt look at her escort.

"Aw. One little dance won't do you any harm," Fitt snorted, being certain that he could apply his charm and attain his desires once they were dancing.

Watching the young man, Marlene felt resentment and annoyance at his behavior. Yet she also saw in it the means by which she would be able to satisfy her curiosity. Knowing that Fitt was a truculent—even dangerous—arrogant bully when he had been drinking, she decided that she could find out how Mark Counter would react if faced by a threatening situation. Fitt fancied himself as being a good roughhouse brawler and was proud of his skill and speed with a gun. In his present condition, provoking him against her escort ought not to be too difficult.

"Even if I did feel like it," Marlene said, selecting her words carefully so that her purpose would not be too obvious, "I've already promised the next dance to Mark."

While that was not the truth, the woman doubted if the blond giant would contradict her. Nor did he. In fact, he never spoke but continued to watch Fitt. Marlene saw her host's son stiffen slightly and direct a glare, which he probably believed to be filled with menace, at Mark.

"He'll change his mind and release you from your promise," Fitt declared. "Won't you, *Mark?*"

Normally the blond giant was an easygoing, sociable, and amiable young man. Conscious of his exceptional strength, he did not let himself become involved in fights unless provoked. However, he had his pride and took exception to the newcomer's attitude and behavior.

Mark still did not know who Fitt might be, but now had sufficient clues to form an opinion of what he was. His accent was well-educated, but Northern rather than Texan. In the absence of further details, Mark thought Fitt might be the son of a carpetbagger who had—like a few of that kind—taken over a ranch. Whoever he might be, he clearly considered himself wild, woolly, full of fleas, and never once curried below the knees. Such an outlook, especially when backed by an overbearing nature and a belly filled with hard liquor, could lead to trouble.

In fact, Fitt was clearly looking for it.

The big blond had no desire to become involved in an unpleasant incident while a guest in a stranger's house. Yet he decided that backing away from his challenger would avail him little or nothing. Also, if he yielded to the man's demands, he would not be able to continue his acquaintance with the woman, and after her comments about Goodnight's possible motives, he wished to do that.

"No," Mark answered. "I *won't.*"

"How do you mean, you *won't?*" Fitt spat out and his right hand went to the ornate Tiffany grips of his Colt.

"Mister," Mark said quietly, watching the other's right forefinger passing through the revolver's exposed trigger guard. "I'm a guest of the Fitts and I don't want any trouble—"

"Maybe you've no choice in it," Fitt pointed out.

"Then it'll be of *your* making," Mark drawled and measured the distance between them with his eyes. "But, mister, if you try to pull that gun, I'll slap your head off your shoulders."

"Try it!" Fitt challenged and stabbed at the holster's operating button.

Despite being ready to respond at Fitt's first hostile gesture, Mark was taken by surprise. He had expected the young man to use the same method as Solly Cole would have when drawing a gun. Instead of pivoting the revolver forward from the grasp of a spring retention clip, Fitt caused the front of the holster to hinge open. So, before the expected movement had happened, he held the weapon.

Two things saved the blond giant. The speed of his own reactions and the fact that Fitt was nowhere near as capable as he imagined.

Whipping down and across, Mark's left hand deflected the weapon as it began to lift in his direction. No less swiftly, his right arm flung the other palm against Fitt's left cheek. While the openhanded slap failed to fulfill Mark's promise, it still proved most effective. Spun around and pitched sideways Fitt lost his hold on the revolver. Luckily, he had not succeeded in drawing the hammer far enough to operate the mechanism. So it clattered to the floor, but failed to fire.

Fitt's whirling, almost graceful, departure was brought to a halt when he collided with the wall of the mansion. Half blinded by tears and wild with rage, he glared at the big blond and the woman. There was a mocking smile on Marlene's lips and it goaded Fitt like the prick of a spur. His right hand disappeared beneath his calfskin vest, to where he carried a Remington Double Derringer tucked into his waistband. He was beyond his assailant's reach this time and felt sure that the other could not hope to come within arm's length before the little hideout pistol was out and lined.

Equally aware of that fact, although he could not see what kind of weapon Fitt was drawing, Mark did not try to advance. Watched by Marlene, who had retreated a few steps, his right hand dipped and rose. There was a rasping of steel on leather, followed by the rapid triple click of a single-action revolver's hammer being drawn to full cock.

Never had Marlene seen such speed. Not even her husband, or Dolman, could have equaled it. Flowing from Mark's offside holster, the long-barreled, ivory-handled Army Colt crashed while held at waist level.

Flying where it had been meant to go, the bullet smacked into the wall not two inches from Fitt's head. While he had done a lot of shooting, it was the first time he had been under fire. He did not find it a pleasant sensation. In fact he received a fright which stiffened him into immobility, the eerie sound of the close-passing lead still ringing in his ears.

"Throw it away!" Mark ordered, cocking the Colt on its recoil and returning its barrel to alignment.

Even as Fitt obeyed, pitching aside his half-cocked Derringer as if it was red hot, he realized that he had had a narrow escape. Inexperienced in practical gunplay as he was, he did not know just how narrow it had been. Many a *pistolero* would have been fired, instead of warning, as long as he had continued to hold the weapon.

Voices were raised in alarm from inside the dining room. The matter between Mark and Fitt might have ended, if it had not been for Marlene. Still annoyed by Fitt's behavior, she wanted him taught an even stiffer lesson and thought that she knew how to bring it about. Standing so that Mark could not see her, she continued to stare at the other young man with an expression of derision.

Seeing how Marlene was looking at him, Fitt was filled with a mixture of rage and humiliation. He watched Mark's revolver return to its holster almost as rapidly, with a twirling motion, as it had appeared. Then he flung himself bodily at the blond giant, ignoring the people who were coming from the French windows.

Instead of trying to avoid the attack, Mark stepped forward as if intending to meet it head-on. At the last moment, with Fitt's hands reaching for him, he swayed his head and torso to the left. As Fitt was carried forward by his impetus, Mark's right fist rammed into his solar plexus. Although the blow had barely traveled six inches, its power was sufficient to halt its recipient in his tracks and bend him at the waist. While big, Fitt's way of life was not the kind to keep him in good condition.

Shooting out his left hand, Mark caught Fitt by the scruff of the neck and gave a heave. Shooting by the big blond, like the cork being blown from the neck of a champagne bottle, Fitt went rushing across the porch. Striking his legs against the wall upon which Marlene had been sitting, he went over as if turning a somersault. Landing flat on his back in a flower bed, he bounced once and then lay still.

Taking no notice of the people who were streaming from the dining room, Marlene stared in open admiration at the blond giant. He had justified, even exceeded, her hopes with the manner in which he had handled Fitt. If she could only bring him round to her way of thinking, he would be a powerful force in her future plans. She had suspected it before and was now even more certain.

Stepping to the wall, ready to take whatever action might be necessary, Mark looked over. One glance told him that he would have no further trouble with the young man, at least not for some time to come. Mark did not know it, but he had vindicated Marshal Grillman's belief that somebody would have to pick up Fitt's toes. He had done so in a most thorough and satisfactory manner.

"I'm right sorry for all the fuss, Mr. Fitt," the big blond said, turning from the wall and looking to where his host was pushing to the front of the crowd. "But this feller," he pointed over and down to his victim's recumbent body, "wouldn't have it any other way."

"What—Who—?" Horatio Fitt spluttered.

"Garvin was most offensive to me," Marlene interrupted, taking the opportunity to strengthen her position with Mark. "Then he started to pick a quarrel and tried to draw on Mr. Counter."

"Garvin!" Fitt Senior yelped. "Is he—?"

"I didn't shoot at him, sir," Mark replied. "Only to come close and scare him into throwing his Derringer away—"

"He'd already pulled his revolver on Mark," Marlene put in.

"Where is he now?" Mrs. Fitt wailed.

"Lying in the garden, ma'am," Mark answered. "I'm real sorry that it had to happen—"

"Mark certainly wasn't to blame for it," Marlene insisted, as Mrs. Fitt ran to the wall.

"I suppose not," Fitt grunted, having no illusions regarding his son's behavior. "If some of you gentlemen will take Garvin to his room, we'll go on with the ball."

"I reckon I'd best be leaving, sir," Mark stated, after four of the guests had complied with their host's request and his wife had gone along to show them where to go.

"You don't have to," Fitt answered, although the tone of his voice suggested that he was not averse to the idea.

"It's kind of late and I'm tired," Mark drawled. "So I'll ask you to thank your lady for an enjoyable evening, say I'm sorry for what happened just now, and get going."

"Where are you staying, Mark?" Marlene inquired, being determined not to lose contact with the blond giant.

"With my kin. Doctor Sandwich and his family."

"They live near to the Belle Grande Hotel, don't they?"

"Yes, ma'am," Mark agreed, guessing what was coming next.

"Then perhaps you'll walk me back there on your way home," the woman suggested. "I didn't bring my coach—"

"It'll be my pleasure, ma'am," the big Texan declared.

Fetching Marlene's cloak and his own white, Texas-style Stetson, Mark escorted her to the hotel. As they walked, she resumed the conversation that had been interrupted by the arrival of Garvin Fitt. From what Mark said, he had given serious consideration to her comment regarding Goodnight's motives. What was more, he appeared doubtful whether it would be possible to drive a herd of cattle to Kansas.

On leaving the blond giant at the door of the hotel, after arranging to take lunch with him and accompany him to the steer-roping contest in which he would be competing, Marlene went upstairs satisfied that she had accomplished something. She felt so elated that she was tempted to waken de Froissart and boast of her achievement. However, she put the idea from her head. If she went to the Creole, he might want to resume their interrupted love-making. The idea did not appeal to her. Not only was she very tired, but even de Froissart—no slouch in such matters—struck her as being pallid and insipid after the man she had just met and, she felt sure, had converted to her cause.

10

I HELPED HIM INTO A GRAVE

"Good morning, Marlene," Pierre de Froissart said, rising as the woman approached the table he was sharing with another man in the hotel's otherwise empty dining room. He indicated his companion, who was also starting to stand up. "I believe you know Cyrus Lonegron."

"We've met," Marlene Viridian answered. "Sit down, please."

Although Marlene had come downstairs, shortly before noon, dressed in a manner which she believed would impress Mark Counter when he arrived to collect her, she had been interested in the man who was talking to the Creole. She knew that Lonegron owned a hide and tallow factory on the mouth of the Brazos River, near to the town of Quintana. Of slightly below middle height, heavily built, with a thick moustache that did little to soften the hard lines of his tanned face, he wore a gray suit, white shirt, and a polka-dot bow tie. Knowing that he had an unsavory reputation, she was intrigued by what might have brought him to Fort Worth. Sufficiently so to decide that she must try to find out.

"Won't you join us?" de Froissart inquired, drawing out a chair.

"I already have an appointment for lunch," Marlene

warned, but sat down. "So I hope you'll excuse me if I have to leave."

"An appointment," the Creole repeated. "Who—"

Seeing the frown which flickered to the woman's face, de Froissart did not finish the question. It had, however, gone by the time she looked at the other man.

"And what brings you to Fort Worth, Mr. Lonegron?" Marlene asked, in a casual tone and as if making idle conversation.

"The same thing as fetched you," the stocky man replied, looking around to make sure that the words would not be overheard. "I don't cotton to this notion of folks taking herds to Kansas any more than you do."

"It certainly won't be to any of our benefit," Marlene conceded cautiously. "But there doesn't seem to be anything we can do about it."

"Your man tried yesterday," Lonegron pointed out.

"I don't follow you," the woman countered, but although she sounded convincingly puzzled, she could not stop herself darting a worried glance at the Creole. "If you mean my husband, he's at home with the—"

"He's likely headed for home by now," Lonegron interrupted. "But he sure as hell won't be there yet."

"Are you suggesting that I'm lying?" Marlene snapped.

"Don't play the innocent with me, Mrs. Viridian," Lonegron warned. "I heard about Dover getting killed and them three fellers trying to jump Dusty Fog. From what's being said, the one who got away could be your husband dressed up to make folks think he's a cowhand."

"Really, Pierre!" Marlene gasped, with well-simulated annoyance, and made as if to thrust back her chair. "Are you just going to sit there—?"

"You do it *real* well, Mrs. Viridian," Lonegron complimented with a sardonic grin. "Fact being, you nearly convinced me that I'm wrong. But don't waste it on me any more. I don't give a damn what Austin did, because I know what he was trying to do. I'm here for the same thing."

"And what might that be?" the woman demanded, sitting down again.

"Making sure that nobody believes Goodnight's notion will work," Lonegron answered. "That's why I wish that Austin had finished Fog off before he lit out!" He raised a hand to silence de Froissart's protest before it could be uttered, looking and speaking to Marlene. "Look, to show you I'm on the level, I'll give you something to use back at me. I've sent men to make sure that Goodnight doesn't arrive with those Eastern buyers. And I've told them to kill him if they have to do it."

"Thank you for being so frank with us," the woman said, in a more friendly tone. "Now I can see why you wish that Fog was dead. If Goodnight doesn't get here, the ranchers will listen to him."

"I don't think they will," de Froissart put in.

"Have you seen him?" Lonegron challenged.

"Yes," the Creole replied. "He doesn't look very impressive—"

"Don't let his size fool you," Lonegron interrupted. "With his Civil War reputation, there's plenty of the ranchers will reckon he's a forty-four caliber man."[1]

"That's true enough," de Froissart admitted, knowing what was meant by the words "a forty-four caliber man." "But, at the moment, the ranchers are interested in whether it's possible to drive herds to Kansas and sell them there, not in Fog's ability as a cavalry officer. They don't see how that will help him when he's working cattle."

"But Fog's speaking for Goodnight," Marlene pointed out. "I saw him last night at the Fitts' ball—"

"And I've been speaking with some of the ranchers he met there this morning," the Creole put in. "They're interested in what Goodnight thinks, but don't believe young Fog knows enough about it on his own account. After all,

1. How this term originated and what it implied is told in: *.44 Calibre Man*.

commanding a company of cavalry doesn't have much in common with working cattle."

"He was Goodnight's segundo on the drive to Fort Sumner," Lonegron reminded the man and woman.

"And, as I pointed out when it was mentioned in the barroom just now," de Froissart replied, "he's also Goodnight's nephew. The general feeling when I left was that there might have been more kin than ability involved in him being made segundo."

"I'd feel happier if Fog wasn't around," Lonegron growled. "But getting rid of him won't be—"

At that moment, there was the sound of laughter and voices in the entrance lobby and footsteps approached the main door of the dining room.

"It might be better if we weren't seen together," Marlene suggested, looking at the stocky man.

"That's right," Lonegron agreed and rose quickly. "I'll see you tonight at the Post Oaks, Pierre."

With that, the man strode to the side door and had gone through it before a small party of ranchers and their wives entered. None of them were known to Marlene and de Froissart and all went to a table by the front window.

"What do you make of Lonegron, Pierre?" Marlene inquired.

"He was telling the truth about why he's here," the Creole stated. "What I didn't like was the way he tied Austin in with Dover's death. If anybody else started thinking that way—"

"Don't worry," Marlene said, sounding more confident than she was feeling. "Harlow will make sure that nobody believes it. We'll—"

"What's wrong?" de Froissart demanded as the woman stopped speaking. He followed the direction in which she was staring and studied the handsome blond giant in expensive, yet functional, cowhand clothing who had just strolled into the dining room. It became obvious that the newcomer was making for their table.

"Hallo, Mark," Marlene greeted, rising and offering her right hand to the big Texan. "I'd like you to meet my husband's partner, Pierre de Froissart. Pierre, this is Mark Counter. We met at the Fitts' ball and I've promised that I'll go to bring him good luck when he rides in the steer-roping contest."

"With Marlene rooting for me," the blond declared, "I don't see how I can lose."

Darting a glance at Marlene, de Froissart shook hands with the big Texan and was impressed. There was a latent power in his grip that suggested exceptional physical strength held carefully under control. What was more, his whole attitude—particularly the way in which he wore his Colts—was that of a very capable fighting man. There, the Creole decided, stood a man who might be a match for Dusty Fog. Perhaps, the Creole concluded, that was why Marlene was taking such an interest in Mark Counter.

*   *   *

Accompanied by the Ysabel Kid and dressed much as he had been during his meeting with Dover and Viridian, Dusty Fog was at that moment entering the office of the town marshal. They found Harlow Dolman present and seated at the desk. While he was unshaven, his clothing looked reasonably clean and neat.

The previous night, after the Kid had returned to the barroom at the Snapping Turtle, Dusty and Marshal Grillman had tried to learn about *Nemenuh* Grift's activities and associates. They had failed to discover anything to help them. On being questioned, Ram Turtle had stated that the man had been alone since his arrival at about midnight. The saloonkeeper had been equally vehement in his declaration that Grift had not previously been in his place. While they were certain that he was lying, there had been no legal, or peaceable, way in which they could prove it.

To have tried to take the matter further would almost certainly have led to more killings. Turtle had been displaying a growing rage and might have thrown discretion to the winds if they had continued to provoke him. Remembering that Grillman had no legal, nor official, status at the Snapping Turtle—and being aware that there were men in Fort Worth who would be delighted to find an excuse to have him removed from office—Dusty had suggested that they left. On taking their departure, the Kid had stated his intention of remaining in the woods and keeping watch. When satisfied that nobody was following them, he had joined his companions and they had returned to the town.

"Howdy, Cap'n Fog, Kid," drawled Grillman, acting in a more formal manner than he would have shown if Dolman had not been there. "The captain here's just got back from chasing that killer."

"We didn't get him," Dolman went on, as two pairs of eyes swung in his direction. "He was heading northeast and we lost him when he crossed the Trinity. My man couldn't find his tracks again, so I thought I'd come back and telegraph the State Police at McKinney to watch for him."

"He was headed *northeast*, huh?" asked the Kid.

"Yes," Dolman agreed and, having noticed the slight emphasis placed on the compass direction he had given, eyed the Indian-dark youngster in a speculative manner. "Which way did you expect him to be going?"

"Ain't done a whole slew of thinking on it," the Kid answered, lying with the attitude of one who was speaking the unvarnished and absolute truth. "Happen I had, though, I'd've reckoned he'd be headed west."

"Why *west?*" Dolman challenged.

"That's where Mr. Dover's spread lies, or so the marshal was telling us," the Kid explained. "Down in Comanche County, which's west of here."

"North *south*west, I'd say," Grillman commented.

"Do *you* think the killer might be one of Do—Mr. Dover's neighbors, marshal?" Dolman inquired, delighted at having been presented with an opportunity to discover if the other peace officer had any suspicions of the truth.

"I'd a notion it might have been, seeing's how they hadn't robbed him after they'd pistol-whipped him," Grillman replied, with an air of unsullied veracity which matched that of the Kid. "Only from what you've just told us, I'm beginning to wonder if maybe I was wrong."

Watching the captain, Dusty wondered if an expression of relief had flickered across his face at the marshal's earlier words. It had come and gone before the small Texan could be sure, being replaced by a blank—yet somehow wary—stare.

"I can't be certain that the man was heading for McKinney," Dolman warned, wanting to keep Grillman thinking along harmless and erroneous lines. "Even if he had come from Comanche County, he'd hardly be likely to head straight back there."

"That's for sure," Dusty agreed. "What did Mrs. Dover say about her husband having enemies, captain?"

"I couldn't ask her," Dolman confessed, although the small Texan had already known roughly what the answer would be. "She was hysterical and not making sense when I went to see her. The doctor said it would be some time before she would be, so I decided not to wait. After all, the trail wasn't getting any warmer."

"I saw her after you'd gone," Grillman remarked, sounding almost apologetic. "She said the feller Cap'n Fog described didn't put her in mind of anybody. But she allows that her husband didn't get on too well with some of his neighbors. Could be one of them hired those yahoos and sent 'em after him."

"That's possible," Dolman declared. "In fact, I think it's a possibility worth investigating."

"I figured it might be," the marshal went on. "But, only being a *local* peace officer, I can't do it."

"I'll see to it for you," Dolman promised, not averse to finding a reason for leaving. "In fact, I'll go along to the telegraph office and send word to the State Police in Comanche to find if it did happen that way."

"That's right obliging of you, captain," Grillman stated.

"I'll do it on the way to the Belle Grande," Dolman offered. "Then I'm going to have a hot bath, a shave, and catch up on the sleep I missed last night. I'd be obliged if you'd send me word if anything turns up, marshal."

"You can count on it," Grillman assured him.

"Well," Dusty said, after Dolman had left the office. "How does it feel to know you've guessed wrong?"

"I don't follow you," the marshal declared.

"That feller was headed to the *northeast,*" the small Texan elaborated. "And Pilar's down to the *south.*"

"Why, sure," Grillman agreed. "From that, it *couldn't've* been Viridian who jumped you."

"Now me, I'm not smart like some's I could name," the Kid stated, favoring his companions with a superior expression. "But I'd say it'd take *real* fancy tracking to follow that feller's trail clear to the Trinity—especially as they'd've had to go at a full gallop to get there 'n' back by now and do most of it in the dark."

"Why didn't *we* think of *that?*" Grillman wanted to know, despite having already drawn a similar conclusion. "Comes to a point, Dolman looked mighty clean, tidy, and refreshed seeing's how he'd been in the saddle all night, riding so far and fast. I was all set to ask how he'd done it. Only he might've took offense, figuring I didn't believe him."

"So he should, for shame," the Kid chided. "Why a captain in good ole Carpetbag Davis's State Police'd no more think of lying than I would."

"Now there's what I'd call a *real* good recommendation of honesty," the marshal scoffed, before growing serious. "Something else's come to mind, though. Couple of times when Mrs. Viridian's been up here without her husband, her and Dolman've been seen out and about with each other. Fact is, I heard's he'd lit out with her like the devil after Ysabel the last time she was here—and that would be the same day's the *Herald* came out with the story about Colonel Charlie's notion."

"You reckon that they rushed down to Pilar so's they could let her husband and his partners know what was coming off?" the Kid inquired innocently. "Why, that'd be almost like saying he was in cahoots with them."

"I've known less likely things," Grillman replied. "Which'd mean that he knowed what Viridian was fixing to do."

"Even if he didn't, knowing the family so well, he'd figure that it could be her husband I was describing," Dusty pointed out. "And, happen he is so all-fired friendly, he wouldn't want anybody thinking along those same lines. So he took out the posse, with men he could trust, and came back to say the feller was heading in just about the opposite direction to Pilar."

"He sure acted jumpy when I asked about the feller going northeast," the Kid admitted.

"Sure," Grillman agreed. "But truthful lil ole you sure showed him that you wasn't figuring on him having gone south."

"You didn't do too bad along those lines yourself," the Kid countered.

"What riles me, though," the marshal growled, losing his levity, "is Dolman thinking we'd be too stupid to see he was lying."

"Let him think what he likes," Dusty replied. "The thing that counts is that he's no idea we suspect Viridian. That's going to be a big help."

"You're real set on getting him, aren't you, Dusty?" Grillman said.

"Not *getting* him," the small Texan objected. "But I have to know if he did kill Mr. Dover. If we're guessing right about why it was done, I feel responsible for it happening."

"How could you be?" the marshal asked.

"It was me who told him how he could get together with

some of his neighbors and share the costs of a drive to Kansas," Dusty explained. "He seemed real eager to try it. If he hadn't been, he might still be alive. Could be I helped him into his grave."

"Hell's fire!" Grillman ejaculated. "Nobody could think *that.*"

"I do," Dusty answered quietly. "And I'll not rest easy until I know the truth of it."

"Getting at the truth's not going to be easy," Grillman warned.

"I know," Dusty conceded. "But we're working on it."

"We?" the marshal repeated, then enlightenment showed on his face. "So that's what—"

The comment went uncompleted, due to the front door of the office opening. A tall, lanky man in worn, cheap town clothes and carrying a buff-colored envelope entered.

"Howdy, Mr. Schelling," Grillman greeted, although his voice held little cordiality. "Is that for me?"

"No, for Cap'n Fog," the man replied. "They told me at the Stockmen's Hotel's I'd find you here, Cap'n."

"Gracias," Dusty drawled, accepting the envelope. He reached into his pocket and produced a ten cent piece. "Here."

"Thank you," the man said, grabbing the coin and scuttling from the office.

"He looked sort of nervous," the Kid remarked.

"Yeah," the marshal agreed, scowling at the door as Dusty opened the envelope and extracted its contents. "I've never trusted him and if I thought he was figuring on selling whatever's in that mess—"

"What's up, Dusty?" the Kid interrupted, reading a change on his *amigo's* face that the marshal could not have detected.

"It's from Uncle Charlie," the small Texan replied. "He says that he won't be able to get here as early as he expected."

"Does he say why?" Grillman growled.

"Only that there's been some delays that he doesn't think were accidental," Dusty answered. "And that I'll have to keep on talking for him until he gets here."

*   *   *

Seeing Harlow Dolman at the main door of the hotel's dining room and catching his signal, de Froissart excused himself and rose. He left Marlene to hold Mark Counter's attention and joined the peace officer in the lobby.

"Who's that with Marlene?" Dolman demanded.

"His name's Mark Counter," the Creole replied and, being unwilling to display his own lack of knowledge regarding the blond giant, went on, "We think that he could be useful in getting rid of Dusty Fog."

"Let's hope he is," Dolman declared. "Because it will have to be done. I just met Schelling from the telegraph office taking a message to Fog. It was to say that Goodnight doesn't think he'll make it for the Convention."

While Marshal Grillman's suspicions had been at least partly justifiable, Schelling had not given the full contents of the message when stopped in the street by Dolman.

"That's great news!" the Creole enthused. "What's happening about Dover's killing?"

"Don't worry," Dolman replied and a contemptuous smile played on his lips. "Grillman hasn't any idea of why he was killed and I've fixed it so that nobody will even think of suspecting Viridian."

11

I HATE A SORE LOSER!

The noose of the thirty-five-foot length of Manila rope—its triple strands laid and plaited extra hard for smoothness and strength—left Mark Counter's right hand and flew toward the head of the fast-moving brown and white long-horn steer.

Having carried its rider into a perfect position to the left of the steer, Mark's bloodbay stallion veered to the right the moment he made his throw. Although a good seventeen hands, the horse moved with speed and agility. Knowing what to expect when the noose had dropped over the six foot spread of horns, the stallion began to whirl inward even before it felt the touch of the rein on the right side of its neck.

Watching the stem of the rope slipping through the honda and closing the noose on the steer's neck, Mark caused his left fingers to draw back lightly on the reins. With the rawhide pigging thong gripped between his teeth, he could not give verbal commands. Nor, so well trained in its duties was the stallion, would they be necessary.

On receiving the expected signal, the huge horse tucked its hind hooves well under its body. Thrusting forward, the front legs braced themselves ready for the shock of the impact and the stallion slid to a halt. Coming down from releasing the rope, Mark's right hand grasped the saddle horn to which it was securely knotted. The left, still holding the reins, rested on top of his mount's neck.

Even as the rope snapped between the two animals, Mark swung his right leg over the cantle of the saddle and started to drop to the ground. With the judges' stopwatches ticking away, not a second could be wasted. His weight and the double hold of his hands combined to give support at the moment of impact.

With a sudden jerk, almost eleven hundred pounds of swiftly moving longhorn was brought to an abrupt halt. Its feet flew from under it and its body struck the ground with a bone-jarring thud. Immediately, the stallion began to haul on the rope so that there would not be an inch of slack to let the steer regain its feet.

Relying upon his mount to prevent the steer from rising, Mark dashed forward. He flung his two hundred and fifty pound body onto the recumbent animal and lay across it. Snatching the pigging thong from his mouth, he caught hold of and dropped a loop around the steer's forelegs just above the hooves. A swift grab with the right hand captured the upper hind leg and drew it to where it could be attached to the ensnared front limbs. With all three secured, he sprang to his feet and raised his right hand.

Cheers and applause rose from the two lines of people who formed a living corridor about a hundred yards wide. Standing roughly in the center, in front of the section of the crowd which held the more influential and important of the spectators, Mark saw one of the judges wave an acknowledgment of his signal. While two of the officials compared the times on their watches, a third hurried forward to check that the steer was fastened securely. Satisfied on that point, he told Mark to set the animal free. Not until it received its master's signal did the bloodbay allow the rope to go slack.

Liberating his noose, the blond giant coiled the rope as he returned to praise the horse. He left the steer to be freed by the men appointed to carry out the task of driving it back into the corral from which it had been released so that it could be roped, thrown, and tied. Leading the big horse, Mark strolled to where Marlene Viridian and Pierre de Froissart were sitting in a hired buggy.

"That was *very* well done, Mark," Marlene praised, echoing the congratulations which were coming from all sides.

Although the term "rodeo" had not yet come into use, county fairs and other such festivities in the cattle country frequently offered contests designed to test the cowhands' skill in various aspects of their work. Mark Counter had just been competing in one of the events.

While being exciting and spectacular, and despite being granted world championship status, steer-roping would not become one of the five standard contests on the professional rodeo circuits. Most organizers would prefer calf-roping as being easier to stage and much less dangerous to the competitors.

The basic purpose of calf- and steer-roping was identical, to pursue, capture, and secure the animal in the shortest time possible. There was one very great difference. In Texas during the mid-1860s, the creature involved was a full grown, half wild longhorn steer, not a Hereford, or some other equally domesticated calf.

"Ladies and gentlemen!" bellowed the barrel-chested owner of the Post Oaks Saloon, who had been selected to make the announcements, on account of his stentorian voice. "Mark Counter has a time of one minute, forty-five seconds!"

"You've won, Mark!" Marlene enthused, as the news was relayed and a roar of applause was raised.

"Good for you," de Froissart went on, thinking of the substantial wager which Marlene had insisted upon him making on their arrival.

Glancing at the Creole, the woman could hardly hold down a smile. For the first time since they had been introduced, he sounded amiable when addressing the blond giant. That could have been due to her having explained her hopes regarding Mark while he was preparing to compete in the event, or because de Froissart was five hundred dollars better off on account of the other's efforts.

De Froissart had grudgingly conceded that Mark's conversation at lunch and while accompanying the buggy to the eastern side of Fort Worth, where the day's events were being held, had convinced him that the big blond would be a useful tool against Goodnight. Not only did Mark doubt that the scheme would be feasible, but he clearly disliked Dusty Fog. The blond giant had complained bitterly about the acclaim which most Texans gave to the young captain whenever the War Between The States was mentioned. From what Marlene and the Creole could make out, Mark considered that he had done at least as much for the Southern cause and, in his opinion, was entitled to be regarded just as highly.

"To hear the ga—folks talk," Mark had said angrily, giving the listening couple a good idea of what was causing his animosity, "you'd think he was the only one who fought against the Yankees. Damn it! There was a whole lot of us who wore the Gray and did plenty of fighting. Only we didn't have one uncle for our colonel and another who was Commanding General to make sure we got promoted and our names in the newspapers."

There had been more in that strain. Apparently a girl Mark had met on his arrival in Fort Worth had expressed a preference for Dusty Fog, on account of his Civil War reputation, and had resisted the big blond's vastly superior physical attributes. To make matters worse, she had belonged to a wealthy family and Mark had had hopes— although he had only hinted at them—of marrying into it.

Listening to Mark's comments on the latter subject, the woman and the Creole had found what they considered to be another point in his favor. He was obviously an ambitious young man with expensive tastes and a craving for wealth. These were factors which ought to make him all the more useful for their purposes. In view of Dolman's news, which de Froissart had given to Marlene in Mark's absence, that might become important.

While the Creole had become satisfied that Marlene might have made a good choice, he was deeply suspicious of her motives. Knowing her as well as he did, he wondered if, in addition to regarding the big blond as a means of removing Dusty Fog, she—unlike the girl—was attracted by his physical attributes. If that should be so, de Froissart could have a very serious rival for her affections.

While satisfied that only Lonegron suspected Viridian of being Dover's killer—and confident that he would not talk as long as he needed their help—Marlene had shared de Froissart's delight at Dolman's information. Backed by the woman's implication that Goodnight had had an ulterior motive for making his suggestion, his failure to arrive could be exploited by them as evidence that he lacked faith in it. There would only be Dusty Fog to contend with and the blond giant could possibly remove him.

"You were right when you said we should bet on you, Mark," Marlene praised.

"Why sure," the big blond admitted. "Don't forget I was betting on me too. I figured on making more than the prize mon—"

"What's Fog doing, talking to the judges?" de Froissart put in, knowing that Mark had wagered fifty dollars that he would win.

Following the direction of the Creole's gaze, Marlene and Mark saw the small Texan, holding the reins of his paint stallion, addressing Horatio Fitt and the other judges. The owner of the Post Oaks Saloon supplied the answer to de Froissart's question.

"Ladies and gentlemen!" he boomed out. "Captain Dusty Fog of the OD Connected wishes to enter the steer-roping competition and, if none of the other contestants have any objections, will ride now."

From various points in the crowd, the men who had
taken part in the event replied that they did not object.
Marlene noticed that Mark was one of the last to give his
consent and concluded that he was not pleased that somebody else should be given the opportunity to try and beat
his time. She also observed that none of the others concerned had displayed a similar hesitation. In fact they appeared eager to find out how the legendary Dusty Fog
would acquit himself in the dangerous and exacting competition. While they all knew of his Civil War reputation,
few of them had any notion of his ability as a cowhand.

Looking about her, from her place among the more important and influential of the spectators, Marlene discovered that the ranch owners were also exhibiting considerable interest. How they reacted to the small Texan as
Goodnight's spokesman might easily depend upon the success he had in carrying out what, within the limitations of
the contest, was a basic piece of a cowhand's work.

Turning her gaze to where Dusty had mounted ready to
begin riding his paint stallion toward the starting line, the
woman decided that there was little reason for concern.
Studying his figure, which seemed even smaller on the
huge horse, she compared him with the men who had pre-
ceded him. Every one had been bigger and heavier, with
Mark Counter the largest of all, and none of them had
come within ten seconds of the blond giant's time. It hardly
seemed likely that the diminutive young Texan could do
better. If his intention was to impress the ranchers, he
would probably do himself more harm than good.

If Marlene had needed further reassurance, it came
from the comments which were passed in her vicinity.
While there had been considerable betting on the other
events, either privately or against the professional gamblers who were mingling with the crowd, nobody seemed
willing to place money on Dusty Fog's chances of beating
the time set up by Mark Counter.

Allowing the big paint to move steadily forward, Dusty

placed the pigging thong between his teeth and unstrapped the rope from the right side fork of his saddle. Knotting its end to the horn, he held the coiled stem and the reins in his left hand. His right hand worked the noose to a suitable size through the honda and he gave it a preliminary twirl over his head. Between his legs, responsive to their instructions and those given by the bit in its mouth, the stallion made a fine picture as it strode out. It clearly knew what would be expected of it and was eager to get started.

Using the restraint he was exerting with the reins to keep the stallion at a collected walk, the small Texan contrived to keep the gate of the corral under observation. It opened and a big *golondrino* steer, its dunnish-brown color merging into black along the back and rump speckled with white blotches, was driven out. For a moment, it stood glaring from side to side and examining the two lines of people. Coming up behind it, a mounted man slapped its rump with a quirt, and giving a snort of fury it started to run toward the open range at the end of the human corridor. It went, tail up and head high, with a speed that none of the better-beefed breeds, which were eventually to replace it, could equal.

Waiting for the steer to attain a rapid pace and pass a predetermined point, Horatio Fitt blew a blast on a whistle and the other two judges started their stopwatches.

Instantly Dusty slackened his pull on the reins. Even before his heels tapped their urgent message against the paint's flanks, he felt its walking pace changing to a galloping gait. The right hind hoof, followed by the right fore and left hind simultaneously, then the left fore—which was termed the leading foot—replaced the four-beat sequence, with the same interval following each successive hoof beat, of the walk.

Having been trained for its work, the great paint sped after the swiftly moving steer and rapidly closed the gap as it approached from the left. Oblivious of the excited yells and shouted comments which came from either side, Dusty

concentrated on what he was doing. The majority of people present were connected in some way with the cattle
industry and he knew that highly critical eyes were following his every move. He refused to let the thought, or the
knowledge of what was at stake, fluster him.

As the stallion drew nearer to its quarry, Dusty reached
his decision on how to handle the situation. He discarded
the thought of going in really close, leaning over the steer's
back, and snaring the forefeet from that position. To do so
would be effective, but was not spectacular enough to suit
his current needs. With that thought in mind, he extended
the size of the noose and started to swing it up to the left
above his head.

"Look at the size of that loop!" a rancher commented,
the words carrying to Marlene's party. "He's going to belly
rope it if he's not careful!"

"What does that mean, Mark?" the woman demanded.

"When the loop's that big, it can pass over the steer's
shoulders and legs," the big blond answered, without taking his eyes from Dusty. "Then it pulls tight around the
belly."

"That's no use, is it?" Marlene asked eagerly, remembering how Mark and the other contestants had roped
their steers around the neck.

"None at all," Mark agreed and, although Marlene did
not notice, there was a note of what might have been anxiety in his voice.

Before there could be any more conversation, they saw
Dusty stand in his stirrups and brace his knees against the
fork of the saddle. Clearly he was preparing to start the
capture.

Although the small Texan had commenced his throw as
if planning a straightforward overhead loop, he made the
cast when the noose was behind his right shoulder. His
right arm whipped forward across the circle it had been
following. At the same moment, the wrist and hand gave
the loop a twist toward the left. Advancing from his fingers,

the rope appeared to stop in midair as it passed over the back of the steer. Then, still as if of its own volition, the loop stood up and rolled to the left until the honda was at the opposite side to its position when the throw began.

Passing down, the reason for the extra wide loop became obvious. It encircled the steer's forelegs. Even as the loop left his grasp, Dusty had guided his mount at an angle. Closing about the trapped limbs, the rope snapped them together and jerked them to the right. Immediately, the paint pivoted into a braced halt. Down crashed the steer, turning in the air to alight on its back.

Dismounting in a manner similar to that used by Mark and the other men, the small Texan sprinted toward the steer. Then the crowd could see where his way of catching the animal improved upon his opponents' methods. With the stallion backing away and pulling on the rope, the steer was rolled on to its left side and its legs pointed toward Dusty. What was more, the front limbs were already held together. It only remained for him to gather the right hind leg, draw it against the trapped pair and make use of the pigging thong. This he did and leapt clear to signal that he had finished.

There was a momentary hush, followed by a growing rumble of applause. It was begun, Marlene realized, by the ranchers and cowhands in the crowd; the men best able to appreciate what they had seen.

"Some belly rope!" a cattleman said to the rancher who had commented disparagingly on the matter. "He knew what he was doing."

"Yep," the erstwhile mocker replied. "He sure knew. And that's a hell of a fast time he made."

Silence dropped as the judges, having conferred, addressed the burly saloonkeeper. The crowd's interest was divided between the officials and the small Texan as he walked toward them leading his big paint stallion.

"Ladies and gentlemen!" the saloonkeeper announced,

bringing everybody's attention to him. "Captain Fog's time was—one minute, *thirty-eight* seconds!"

Delighted approval greeted the words, expressed by shouts and ringing Rebel war yells which included the battle cry of Dusty's regiment, "Yeeah! Texas Light!" Clearly many of the spectators were jubilant because their Civil War hero had proven himself highly capable in another field. Disturbed by what she was hearing and seeing, Marlene wondered how Mark was accepting his defeat. Glancing his way, she found that a tight-lipped, angry scowl had come to his handsome face.

After receiving the congratulations of the judges and acknowledging Governor Davis's compliments, Dusty looked around until his eyes came to rest on the blond giant. Dropping the paint's reins, the small Texan left it ground-hitched and strolled toward his rival. To Marlene, it seemed there was an extra jaunty swagger in his walk. Apparently Mark felt the same way, for his frown deepened.

"That was a real good ride you made, feller," Dusty declared, in tones of jovial and slightly condescending praise which the woman was sure would further infuriate the big blond. "I was hard pushed to beat it."

"You'd've been even harder pushed happen you'd been after a fresh steer and not one that'd been out before," Mark replied, sounding surly and ignoring the hand which Dusty had extended.

The words had carried to the nearest of the crowd and drew a low mutter of disapproval. From the comments, it was obvious that few of the listeners agreed with Mark's charge. Clearly they, like Marlene, knew that the *golon-drino* steer had made its first appearance when Dusty tackled it and had not been used previously.

Letting out an indignant snort, Dusty allowed his hand to drop and he stated loudly, "I hate a sore loser!"

"Why you short—!" Mark began and lunged forward with his left fist hurling at the small Texan's head.

Jumping aside, so that the big blond's blow missed and

he blundered by, Dusty pivoted into a kick. Fortunately for its recipient, the small Texan's aim was off. Instead of his boot's toe driving into Mark's kidney region, the front of his shin bone struck the small of the blond's back. So, while he was propelled onward for a few steps, Mark was not seriously injured.

Bringing himself to a halt, the blond giant turned to find his assailant approaching. Around and up flashed Mark's right arm, flinging a backhand blow which caught Dusty on the right cheek and spun him away at a tangent.

Masculine shouts and feminine screams rose as the two young men rushed at each other. However, nobody offered to intervene. Making use of his extra height and reach, the blond giant shot out his hands to catch hold of the lapels of Dusty's calfskin vest. Then, to the watching people, it seemed that the force of Mark's weight had knocked Dusty backward from his feet.

Nothing could have been further from the truth. Apparently confident of his superiority in size and weight, Mark had attacked in a manner which left him wide open to receive a *jujitsu yoko-wakare,* "lateral separation," throw.

Catching Mark by the right bicep from the outside with his left hand, while his right came up to grab the shirt's sleeve below the left armpit, Dusty deliberately—but apparently accidentally—allowed himself to go down. He landed on the left side of his back, drawing the bigger man forward and off balance. Thrusting himself against Mark's advanced right leg so as to block the movements of its ankle, Dusty pushed with his thighs and drew downward on the right arm. Although Dusty released his right hand's grasp, he kept hold with the left as his assailant was compelled to flip over his recumbent, yet far from helpless body. There was a yell of pain from Mark as he landed on his right shoulder, was liberated, and rolled away.

Followed by two of his deputies, Marshal Grillman burst through the crowd without a thought for the quality of the various people he had shoved out of his way. He flung himself forward, grabbing Dusty by the arms as the small Texan leapt up ready to continue the fight. Although the deputies were prepared to restrain Mark, the need to do so did not arise. Sitting up, the big blond seemed to be in considerable pain.

"M—My shoulder!" Mark gasped, clutching at it and keeping his head bent forward as if unwilling to let anybody see how he was suffering. "I—I think it's—it's broken!"

12

HE'LL STILL BE
USEFUL TO US

"There you are," Doctor Samuel Sandwich said, adjusting
the sling which he had fixed to support Mark Counter's
right arm. "That ought to do it."

On examining his nephew's shoulder at the contest
ground, the doctor had been surprised and puzzled by the
extent of its injury. However, deciding what needed to be
done, he had said that the shoulder was merely strained
and not broken. Then he had declared that Mark must be
taken to his home so that he could give the injury proper
attention. Marlene Viridian had insisted that Mark should
ride there in her buggy. What was more, she had accompanied him and had left de Froissart to return with friends.

Delivering Mark to the Sandwich family's home, with
the doctor following and leading the bloodbay stallion,
Marlene had suggested that, if he felt up to it, they might
dine together that evening. Then she had left him in his
uncle's care. At seven o'clock, washed, shaved, and dressed
as he had been when attending the Fitts' ball, the big blond
had asked Sandwich to fix his shoulder so that he could
keep the appointment.

The office's door opened and, considering who entered,
the response from Sandwich, or more particularly Mark,
would have amazed Marlene if she had been present.

"I sure hope that sling's not for real," Dusty Fog remarked, glancing at the window to make sure that the drapes were drawn.

"It's not," the burly, gray-haired, cheerful-looking doctor replied. "But the next time you pair are planning to pull a game like that this afternoon, I'd be obliged if you'd let me in on it. I didn't know what the hell to make of it when you started fighting. And it's not as if *my* side of the family's such ready liars as the Counters."

"You didn't do too badly at it, sir," Dusty declared.

"I'm not sure whether that's a compliment or not," Sandwich protested. "And I'd still like to know why you did it."

"It's easy enough explained," Mark drawled. "You know I'm pretending to have a dislike for Dusty so that I get Marlene's and de Froissart's confidence."

"I know it," the doctor agreed.

"Well," the big blond went on, "this way I'm fixed so that they won't expect me to go up against him with a gun."

"It could have come to that," Dusty continued. "So I took the chance that Mark would guess what I wanted and go along with it."

Learning of Mark's conversation with Marlene, on returning to the Stockmen's Hotel after visiting the Snapping Turtle Saloon, Dusty had been pleased that he had not sent for the big blond to leave the ball and join them. He had seen a way in which he might be able to discover what, if anything, the partners of the Pilar Hide & Tallow Company were planning, and perhaps obtain proof that Viridian had been Dover's murderer.

Having made a detour to visit one of his uncles who ran a ranch in Lampasas County, Mark had not arrived with Dusty and the Ysabel Kid. Nor had they disclosed their association with each other. Dusty had guessed that there might be attempts at disrupting belief in Goodnight's ideas and had felt that the blond giant would be more useful as an apparently uncommitted visitor. So Mark had let it be known that he was attending the Convention on behalf of his father. That was true enough, but Big Rance had already decided Goodnight was correct and had started making preparations for driving a herd to Kansas.

In a year's time, such a deception would not have been possible. By then, Mark Counter's name would have become almost synonymous with Dusty Fog, the OD Connected ranch and Ole Devil Hardin's floating outfit.[1]

Fortunately for the success of Dusty's intentions, there were few people in Fort Worth who were aware that Mark worked for the OD Connected and they could all be relied upon not to betray the fact. Not that Mark's task was any sinecure. If his secret should leak out, the very least that would happen would be that he would lose Marlene's and de Froissart's confidence. It might also mean, especially if he had gathered information that they would try to have him killed. There had, as Mark had told his uncle, also been the danger that Marlene was hoping to use him as a means of removing Dusty. The fight and its aftermath had lessened the chances of it coming about.

"I didn't know you planned to enter the steer-roping contest, Dusty," the doctor remarked.

"I *didn't* at first, although I brought my mount along hoping I'd have time to go in for the cutting horse contest and run the paint in the Three Miles Stakes," the small Texan replied and went on to show that his views on the feelings of the ranchers toward him matched those expressed by de Froissart. He finished, "But when I got the message that Uncle Charlie won't be here as soon as he'd hoped, I figured I'd best start convincing folks I'm more than just a pretty fair cavalry captain."

"Is Colonel Charlie in trouble?" Mark demanded.

"Some," Dusty admitted. "But Lon's riding relay out toward Sulphur Springs, which's where the message was sent from, to see if he can lend a hand."

1. New readers can find details of Mark Counter's career in Appendix 3.

"Does Colonel Charlie know he's coming?" Mark asked.

"I haven't sent word," Dusty replied. "That way Lon'll have surprise on his side."

"You mean that somebody in Fort Worth might have been responsible for Charlie's trouble?" Sandwich suggested.

"It's possible," Dusty agreed.

"Marlene and de Froissart?" Mark growled.

"Them, or somebody else," Dusty answered. "Rupe Grillman allows that Lonegron from Quintana's in town. There could be other hide and tallow men around who we don't know about. Or it's maybe somebody else who's wanting to stop Uncle Charlie getting here."

"Maybe I should forget this sling," Mark hinted.

"Why?" Dusty wanted to know.

"The folks who're trying to stop Colonel Charlie could get the notion that you'll be listened to, even if he doesn't arrive," the blond giant explained. "And the easiest way to see you don't'll be to kill you."

"It's likely," Dusty conceded.

"You won't have Lon to watch your back," Mark reminded him.

"That's a chance I'll have to take," Dusty replied. "And, happen it is Mrs. Viridian's bunch figuring on doing it, you could find out and let me know."

"Assuming that they still figure you're worth knowing, boy," Sandwich pointed out. "After what happened when you tangled with Dusty, they could reckon you're not man enough to take him out of the deal."

"There's that to it," Mark exclaimed hopefully. "What do you reckon about it, Dusty?"

"You could be right, doctor," the small Texan decided. "But most folks I heard talking figured that Mark getting his shoulder 'hurt' was an accident and that I might have been lucky it happened."

"You mean that he tripped over you after he'd pushed

you down," Sandwich elaborated. "It certainly looked that way."

"Well it wasn't!" Mark said emphatically. "I've seen Dusty and Betty Hardin[2] pull that kind of throw and figured letting him use it would be the best way to get 'hurt' without looking as if I'd been licked."

"And you guessed what Mark wanted you to do?" Sandwich asked Dusty. "Or had you planned it in advance?"

"We hadn't," Dusty answered. "But I guessed what Mark was setting himself up for when he took hold that way. We're lucky not many folks know *jujitsu*. Anybody who did would have expected me to let go of his right arm once he was going over. And if I'd had to, that sling would have likely been for real."

"I wouldn't've been in too good shape happen it'd been your toe and not the shin that hit me," the blond giant went on.

Sandwich favored the two blonds with admiring glances. Despite their youth, they were proving themselves shrewd, smart-thinking, and capable. Not only had they dealt with a problem before it had arisen, but without discussion or rehearsal they had "fought" in a most convincing manner and one perfect for their requirements.

"Anyway, the lady doesn't look like she's backing off," the doctor said. "She's asked you to have dinner with her."

"Why sure," Mark drawled. "So we'll have to see what comes off next. But I wish I didn't have to keep acting like I am."

"I thought you looked real natural." Dusty grinned, knowing his big *amigo* was nothing like the character he was portraying for Marlene's benefit.

"I hope Old Devil feels the same way," Mark replied. "You mind how he told us we could spend money if we had to and he'd give it back when we got home?"

2. Betty Hardin: Ole Devil Hardin's granddaughter and Dusty's cousin, who had also been taught *jujitsu* and karate by Tommy Okasi.

"That's what he said," Dusty agreed. "He won't object to you buying dinner for the lady."

"How about that fifty dollars I lost betting that I'd win the steer-roping?" Mark wanted to know.

"*Fifty* dollars?" Dusty echoed.

"You said for me to make it look like I enjoyed throwing money around," the blond giant pointed out. "And, anyways, it's all *your* doing that *I* lost."

"Put that way," Dusty sighed, "I'll have to see you get it back."

"Now you know why I like working for the OD Connected," Mark told his uncle. "What other spread'd *encourage* the hands to gamble. And where else could I get paid for hitting the segundo?"

*   *   *

A far less amicable meeting was taking place in de Froissart's room at the Belle Grande Hotel. Sitting on the bed, the Creole looked from where Dolman was lounging against the window to Marlene as she angrily paced the floor.

"All I'm saying is that Counter didn't show to any advantage when he tangled with Fog," de Froissart stated, but in a placating manner.

As always, opposition to Marlene's beliefs or wishes was making her even more determined to go ahead with the course she had set for herself. Even while making the arrangements to have dinner with Mark Counter, she had been dubious about his further value to her schemes. Her determination to continue, even expand, the acquaintance had increased when she had received a message to join de Froissart in his room. On her arrival, she had found the Creole and Dolman to be in a critical frame of mind. They had begun by commenting upon Dusty Fog's success in the steer-roping contest and of the interest it had aroused among previously doubtful ranchers. Then de Froissart had complained about Mark's attitude and apparently poor showing against the small Texan in the fight.

"He tripped when he knocked Fog over and landed awkwardly," Marlene protested, conveniently overlooking that the suggestion had come from Mark. "Anybody could see that! If it hadn't happened, he would have thrashed Fog as easily as he beat Garvin Fitt."

"And now he's got a badly strained shoulder," Dolman put in. "His *right* shoulder too. So his gun hand's no use."

"He wears *two* guns!" Marlene reminded the men and the note of asperity became more pronounced in her voice.

"I've seen quite a few men who do," Dolman replied in a harsh tone that showed his resentment of her attitude. "But most of them only carry the left hand gun as a reserve."

"Well I think he'll still be useful to us!" Marlene snapped, but did not specify how. Instead, she stalked across the room. "It's time I was going to meet him."

"What do you make of *that?*" de Froissart inquired, after the woman had gone out, slamming the door behind her.

"She seems set to keep him around," Dolman replied.

"Yes," the Creole agreed. "But what's behind it?"

"I'm not sure," Dolman admitted. "It's not because she hopes he'll be able to influence other ranchers against Goodnight. After this afternoon, there's no hope of *that.*"

"And with his gun hand useless, she can't expect him to face up to Fog," de Froissart went on. "I don't like it."

"Or me," Dolman conceded and noticed the speculative manner in which the Creole began to study him. Wishing to divert any suspicions the other might be harboring, regarding his own interest in Marlene's relationship with the blond giant, he continued. "But she's right. Counter could still be useful to us."

"In what way?" de Froissart wanted to know.

"I think Fog should be killed, whether Goodnight arrives for the Convention or not," Dolman explained. "Especially after this afternoon."

"So do I," the Creole admitted, thinking of the comments he had heard passed between ranchers who had pre-

viously been uncertain regarding the small Texan's knowledge of the cattle business. "The trouble's going to be
finding somebody to do it."

"I've already seen Roxterby," Dolman began.

"He won't face Fog!" de Froissart protested.

"I never thought he would," Dolman replied. "But he's
game to bushwhack him from a dark alley one night. And
when it happens, we can lay the blame on Counter."

* * *

"Look at that short-grown son of—!" Mark Counter
growled, halting the words as if suddenly realizing that they
might be offensive to the ears of his companion. "Just
watch him sucking up to those ranchers."

Having had their dinner, Marlene Viridian and the
blond giant had gone on to a reception at the Stockmen's
Hotel. They were in the barroom. It did not usually accept
ladies, but an exception had been made for the evening.
Although the Governor had not yet arrived, there was a
fair-sized crowd in the room. Looking about him, Mark
had noticed that the people were forming into groups. His
words had come on seeing Dusty Fog standing with a party
of prosperous-looking ranch owners at the counter. Near
to them, de Froissart and Dolman were clearly listening to
what was being said despite appearing to be engrossed in
their own conversation.

"I hope that there won't be any more unpleasantness
such as we had this afternoon," Marlene said severely.

"There won't as far as I'm concerned," Mark replied
and gestured with his left hand toward the sling. "I can't do
much with this. Blast it! If I hadn't tripped—"

"I shouldn't let it worry you," Marlene told him. "Come
on. There are some men here I think you'd like to meet."

Listening to the conversation which followed, Mark decided that Marlene had been correct although the reason
he found the men interesting was not what Marlene supposed.

In addition to the other details, while Mark had been

competing in the steer-roping contest, de Froissart had pointed out several ranchers who were dubious about Goodnight's claims. Having seen a small group of them, she steered Mark in their direction. One had delivered cattle to the Pilar Hide & Tallow Company's factory and she used that point to intrude into their conversation. After Mark had been introduced, Marlene guided the talk to Goodnight.

"I'm damned if I reckon it can be done!" declared a burly rancher who wore the uniform of a Confederate States' cavalry officer, except that it had civilian buttons and no insignia.

"Goodnight's a pretty fair cowman, though," a second of the group commented.

"So he should be!" the burly man sniffed. "He had four years at it while some of us was away fighting the Yankees."

Hearing the low mutter of agreement, Mark saw one reason for the group's reluctance to accept a scheme originated by Goodnight.[3] Although a loyal Texan, he had not fought for the South in the War. Instead, he had served with Captain Jack Cureton's Company of Texan Rangers. They had helped to protect the homes of the men away fighting on both sides against Indians, Mexican bandits and renegade whites. However, some people—like the burly rancher and his companions—had a dislike bordering on active hatred for any man who had not worn the cadet-gray uniform of the Confederate States' Army.

"What was it you were saying about Goodnight's idea, Mark?" Marlene asked.

"Huh?" the big blond grunted.

"You remember," the woman prompted. "About why he

3. Charles Goodnight's title "Colonel" was honorary, awarded by his fellow Texans for his courage, ability as a leader, and skill as a fighting man. Dusty Fog's youth prevented him from being granted the same honorific, although he attained it in later years.

might be so eager to get other people to try to reach Kansas with their herds."

Realizing what Marlene meant, Mark found himself on the horns of a dilemma. He did not wish to repeat the suggestion she had made to him regarding Goodnight's possible motives. It would be accepted willingly by his audience, who were sure to pass it along as being true. Others, wavering in the balance, might choose to believe it and decide against trying to reach the new markets. Certainly such a suggestion would arouse controversy and could easily lead to open hostility, for Goodnight had many friends who would bitterly resent such an implication.

Fortunately, the onus of replying was removed from the blond giant.

Even as Marlene stopped speaking and waited expectantly for Mark to carry on, Garvin Fitt walked in. The group to which Marlene had attached the big blond was standing in the center of the barroom, directly in front of the main entrance. So Fitt could hardly avoid seeing Mark as he entered. What was more, going by his lurching gait and reddened face, Fitt was at least as drunk as on their previous meeting.

The moment Mark saw that Fitt's eyes were on him, paying great attention to the sling he was wearing, he saw a possible solution to his problem. Nor did he need to do anything to arouse the other's animosity. Recognition showed on Fitt's face, being replaced by an expression of hatred. Scowling, he slouched forward and, moving slowly, Mark turned toward him.

"It looks like you've run up against somebody who wasn't too drunk to defend himself," Fitt announced in carrying tones, teetering to a halt. However, having learned his lesson, he did so before he had come within reaching distance of the blond giant's hands.

The words had been sufficiently loud to be heard all around the room. Conversations were brought to an end. Marlene and the ranchers with whom she had been speaking looked from Fitt to Mark and, reading the signs, began to draw away. At the bar, Dusty's party, de Froissart, and Dolman fell silent and turned their respective attentions to the center of the floor.

"Well," Mark replied, more quietly but still being audible to the other occupants of the room. "That's one thing I wouldn't need to worry about where you're concerned."

"You've got a real big mouth!" Fitt spat out and his right hand dropped to close around the butt of his Colt. "And I don't like i—"

"Garvin!" Marlene snapped. "Don't be a fool!"

Partly blaming the woman for what had happened to him the previous night—and not without justification—Fitt had turned some of his hatred in her direction. Hearing her speak, he swung his head to glare at her.

"Isn't it time you started remembering you're marri—!" Fitt began.

Taking advantage of the interruption, Mark stepped forward. While he was proficient at drawing and shooting with his left hand, he did not attempt to do either. Instead, he reached and grabbed Fitt by the throat.

Fingers which felt like the steel jaws of a bear trap closed on the young man's neck, choking off the remainder of his speech. Letting out a strangled croak, he involuntarily stabbed his forefinger onto the holster's stud. However, as the front sprang open, his hand left the butt in an attempt to free himself from Mark's grasp and the weapon fell harmlessly to the floor.

Giving Fitt no chance to recover, or free himself, Mark shook him like a terrier dealing with a rat. Then the big blond thrust him backward. Reeling, Fitt somehow managed to retain his balance and remained on his feet. As he came to a halt, he cursed and flung himself forward. Landing belly down on the floor, he grabbed the butt of the Colt with his right hand.

Knowing the kind of man he was dealing with, Mark did not hesitate. His left foot raised and its high heel stamped

on the back of Fitt's hand, pinning it to the floor. A screech
burst from Fitt as he felt the pressure crushing his flesh
and bones against the uneven, unyielding butt of the revolver.

At the bar, Dolman reached a decision. He had guessed
that Mark might be a threat to his hold on Marlene and
saw the opportunity to remove him. At the same time Dolman hoped that he might regain something of the favor he
had lost by his refusal to make Ram Turtle forget young
Fitt's gambling debts, as had been suggested by his father.
To have done so, or even attempted it, would have lost the
peace officer a useful source of income. Particularly as the
saloonkeeper was furious about the visit paid to him by
Dusty Fog, the Ysabel Kid, and Marshal Grillman, about
which Dolman could do nothing.

With that in mind, Dolman liberated and produced his
Colt. He was sure that, when challenged, the blond giant
would give him an opportunity to shoot in "self-defense"
while "resisting arrest." Nor, in view of Counter's behavior
that afternoon, would his death be the cause of too much
adverse comment. So Dolman moved from the counter
and started to raise his weapon.

Having caught Dolman's draw being made from the corner of his eye, Dusty guessed what the other was planning
to do. Which placed the small Texan in a difficult position.
He could not allow his *amigo* to be killed, but had to prevent it without letting their friendship be suspected.

Thinking fast, Dusty thrust himself forward at an angle
which placed him between Mark and Dolman. Even as his
right hand fetched out and cocked the left side Colt, he felt
the muzzle of the peace officer's weapon touching his
spine.

"Back off!" Dusty ordered, without turning or stepping
aside, lining his revolver at the big blond.

Taking his foot from Fitt's hand, Mark twisted his torso.
He saw Dolman behind the small Texan and realized what
must have happened. However, he did not forget to play

his part. Looking down, he saw that Fitt was crouching and nursing the injured hand. So he swung toward Dusty.

"You again!" Mark growled. "One of these days, you'll push your nose into somebody else's affairs and get it blown off."

13
IT'S BETTER THAN BEING IGNORED

Looking at the broken thread, which had been whole when he had fastened it with pins between the jamb and the bottom of the door, Dusty Fog knew that he had had a visitor in his absence. It was not the hotel's maid, for she had finished her work before he had left to have lunch with some ranchers.

It was the morning after Dusty had saved Mark's life. The big blond's pretense of being furious over Dusty's intervention had been so convincing that nobody suspected the truth. Instead, there had been considerable relief shown and expressed when Marlene Viridian had suggested that she and Mark go elsewhere. After they had gone, Dusty had contrived to prevent Dolman from guessing that he had stepped deliberately between him and Mark.

The rest of the evening had been uneventful, with only one disturbing note as far as Dusty was concerned. It had begun, in fact, before Mark's trouble with Fitt. When the subject of Kansas had been brought up, one of the ranchers had asked if there was any truth in the rumor he had heard that Colonel Goodnight might not be attending the Convention. Dusty had replied that, to the best of his knowledge, his uncle would be there and the matter had been forgotten due to Fitt's arrival.

After Mark's departure, the conversation had been resumed. There had been one matter upon which Dusty could not shed much light. On being questioned about an actual shipping point, he was unable to give precise information. While he knew that Goodnight was considering Abilene, he did not feel that he should go into detail regarding his uncle's hopes in that respect. So he had been compelled to restrict himself to saying that he doubted if the problems of loading and transporting the cattle would prove insurmountable. He had realized that doing so did nothing to strengthen his arguments, but had no other choice. To have told the ranchers how Goodnight believed the town would be developed, then to find that it had not happened, would ruin all chances of the rest of the scheme being accepted.

However, Dusty had discovered that his audience was more inclined to listen to his own comments on the business of handling a large herd with a small number of men. While they had not yet been won over completely, there had been a noticeable improvement and he was determined that it should continue.

That morning, with Marshal Grillman's assistance, Dusty had met Mark. Ostensibly they had been summoned to the marshal's office so that they could be warned that no further trouble between them would be tolerated. Dolman had been present during the interview, but had been distracted by Grillman as Dusty had passed a note to Mark while they were being "compelled" to shake hands and forget their differences. Dusty had asked his *amigo* to try and discover whether Marlene and de Froissart had started the rumor that Goodnight would not be at the Convention. After Mark and Dolman had taken their departures, the small Texan had made a similar request to Grillman.

Returning to the hotel, Dusty had been invited to have lunch with the men he had met the previous night. After the meal, during which he had been asked how he regarded his chances in the bucking horse event that afternoon, he had found that the precautions which he had taken against unwelcome visitors were justified.

Looking each way along the passage, to make sure that he was not being observed by the occupants of the other rooms, Dusty drew and cocked his left hand Colt. Then, with his right hand, he unlocked and thrust open the door. Going in fast, with his weapon's barrel sweeping in an arc before him, he was ready to start shooting. The need to do so did not arise, for the room was empty and apparently undisturbed.

Twirling the Colt back into its holster, Dusty closed the door. He made a thorough examination of his quarters, but could find no trace of them having been searched. Yet he felt sure that somebody had entered during his absence. Which meant that the unannounced visitor must have had a good reason for taking the risks involved by doing so. He discounted the possibility of robbery, for all his property appeared to be intact and nothing was missing.

Frowning with concentration, Dusty glanced at one of the fixtures which the Stockmen's Hotel offered with their most frequent type of client in mind. Knowing that a saddle was a vitally important factor in a Texas cattleman's life and being aware of the importance he attached to its safe keeping, the management had placed in each room an inverted V-shaped wooden structure known as a "burro." That allowed the occupant to leave his saddle in safety, instead of having to lay it on its side in a corner or hang it by its horn in the wardrobe.[1]

Crossing to the burro, Dusty reached out his right hand. He would need the saddle to compete in the bucking horse event and meant to carry it to the corral at Mulcachy's livery barn, where the contest was to take place.

---

1. No Texan would ever stand his saddle on its skirts, throw it down, or otherwise abuse it.

A thought struck the small Texan as his hand touched the horn. His participation in the event was known. It would be a good opportunity for somebody to try to remove him and to make the attempt look like an accident.

Dusty started to go over the saddle with a keen-eyed scrutiny. The most likely parts to have been damaged were the girth-straps, or the latigo, which were used to secure the front girth to the saddle's rigging ring. Examining them and the spacer strap which held the girths apart, he could find nothing to suggest they had been tampered with. Nor had the sheepskin lining of the skirt. The *rosaderos,* wide leather shields sewed to the backs of the stirrup leathers, and the leathers themselves were equally unmolested. To make certain, Dusty took the saddle from the burro and placed it on the floor. Setting his foot on each *rosadero* in turn, he gripped the wide wooden foot supports with his hands. Exerting his not inconsiderable strength, he tested the strength of the leather and the metal pins upon which the supports were connected to the straps.

Despite everything appearing to be satisfactory, Dusty could not shake off the feeling that all was far from well. Then a thought struck him. Moving the latigo, he looked at the rigging ring at the front of the saddle. A low hiss burst from him as he saw that the metal had been cut through, probably by a hacksaw. An examination showed that the girth ring at the rear had been treated in an identical fashion, as had their mates on the other side.

Dusty felt as if he had been touched by a cold hand as he set the saddle back on the burro.

If he had not fastened the thread across the door, a trick which he had learned from Belle Boyd, the Rebel Spy, he would not have become suspicious. Instead, he would have taken the saddle and used it in the bucking horse event. Once a horse had started pitching and fighting, the rings would have opened. When the cinches and latigo were liberated, the saddle would have come off. In which case, he might have counted himself lucky to escape with nothing more than a few broken bones.

There was a knock on the door. Even before Dusty had turned, without the need for conscious thought, he held a cocked Colt in his right hand.

"Who is it?" Dusty called, having crossed the room.

"Could be Robert E. Lee," replied Grillman's voice. "But I wasn't born that lucky."

Lowering the Colt's hammer onto the safety notch between two of the cap-nipples of the cylinder, Dusty holstered it and opened the door.

"Schelling won't come out truthful and admit he sold the message he fetched from Colonel Charlie," the marshal announced with preliminaries as he entered. "Much less say who he sold it to."

"That's about what we expected," Dusty pointed out.

"Sure," Grillman agreed, then eyed Dusty in a speculative manner. "It's not my way to be nosy, but I was wondering if you allus answer the door with a gun in your fist?"

"Only when I'm in a town where somebody's trying to kill me," Dusty replied, guessing that the marshal had heard the distinctive triple clicking as he had brought the weapon to full cock despite the door being between them.

"Now who-all'd want to do a mean thing like that?" Grillman inquired, but there was a hardness under the levity. "And how was they figuring on doing it?"

"Like this," Dusty explained, leading the way and displaying the damaged rings on the saddle.

"Whooee!" the marshal cried. "If you'd been using this on a hoss with a belly full of bedsprings—"

"Why sure," Dusty drawled, as the words died away.

"It looks like somebody doesn't want you around," Grillman remarked. "Oh well, it's better than being ignored."

"There's some might think so. Only I'm not one of them."

"Shucks. I allus thought you'd got a sense of humor."

"Why thank you 'most to death," Dusty growled. "Now I know how that feller Job in the Good Book must've felt."

"I'd never've give you credit for having even *seen* the Good Book," Grillman countered. "Who-all do you reckon done it?"

"I *never* thought *you* had a sense of humor," Dusty declared. "Now I'm sure of it. How the hell do I know who did it? That's what the good tax-paying citizens of Fort Worth're paying you-all to find out."

"I'll ask around the hotel—" the marshal offered.

"There's no rush," Dusty told him. "Fact being, we might learn more by not letting on we've found out about the saddle."

"How?"

"Somebody's expecting me to get thrown. Could be they're even betting money on it. So let's make 'em think I'm headed for a fall and see what happens."

"Might's well," Grillman conceded. " 'Specially's I can't figure out any other way of learning who done it."

"The good tax-paying citizens of Fort Worth—" Dusty began.

"Are getting more than their money's worth, what they pay me," Grillman countered, having guessed what was coming. "There's only one thing, though. What're you going to do for a saddle? You sure as hell-and-a-half can't use that one, way it is, and there's no time to get it fixed."

"I'll ask Festus Mulcachy to lend me his," Dusty answered. "Joe Gaylin made it and it's enough like mine for us to fool anybody who doesn't come too close."

Taking up his saddle, Dusty swung it onto his left shoulder. On leaving the room together, the marshal locked its door and fixed another piece of thread in place. Going downstairs, they separated in the lobby and Dusty made his way to the livery barn.

On arriving, Dusty found the owner and requested a few words in private. On seeing the damage to the small Texan's saddle, Mulcachy swore luridly and asked how he could help. He agreed to lend Dusty his saddle without hesitation. Not only had he served in the Texas Light Cavalry during the War, but he owed Ole Devil Hardin a very big favor. In addition to helping Dusty in that way, Mulcachy promised to try to find out if there was any significant betting.

Dusty was to make two rides that afternoon and his reputation as a cavalryman had placed him among the favorites. However, neither Grillman nor Mulcachy managed to find anybody who was wagering in such a manner that he appeared to be certain the small Texan would lose. Attending with Marlene and de Froissart, Mark reported—during a clandestine meeting with the marshal—that both had placed fair sums of money on Dusty; which suggested that they were not involved in the plot.

The first horse allocated to Dusty was a roman-nosed, small and ugly bay gelding. While it appeared docile as it allowed itself to be roped, saddled, and bridled, Dusty was not fooled by its apparently placid nature. Which proved to be fortunate. Once he was astride it and the blindfold had been removed, the bay proved to be a vicious fighter. It was what was known as a close-to-the-ground pitcher. Never leaping high, it moved fast, kicking sideways with its hind quarters, shaking its head from side to side, and contorting its body in an unending attempt to so befuddle its rider that he lost all sense of timing and direction. With such a mount, it was all too easy for the man on its back to miss track of it completely and find himself ploughing up dirt with his chin. That did not happen in Dusty's case, but he had several bad moments before the battle came to its end.

Dismounting and acknowledging the applause of the crowd, Dusty could not help thinking what would have happened if he had failed to discover the damage to his saddle and had fastened it to such an animal.

Making the final ride of the day, Dusty knew that he would win the event if he succeeded in completing it. He took on a big, rangy, yellowish claybank[2] stallion which fought the rope and needed to be eared down, with a man gripping each ear between his teeth so that pain would make it stand still, before it could be saddled. It proved to be a very different proposition to the bay, being a cloud hunting high roller, bounding high and slamming down hard, alternating the leaps by rearing wildly, vaulting upward, and pawing the air with its forefeet.

Finding that such tactics failed to dislodge Dusty, the claybank tried runaway pitching. After dashing in a straight line for about fifty yards at a gallop, it flung itself five feet into the air. Alighting on stiff legs, it struck the ground heavily and with considerable force. The rapid forward motion had ceased so abruptly that the stallion seemed to be thrusting itself backward as it reached the ground. Although Dusty was thrown against the fork of the saddle, then back onto the cantle, he remained aboard it.

The fight ended soon after the claybank had hurled itself in blind fury at the rails of the corral. Seeing the danger, Dusty quit its back an instant before the collision. Landing on his feet, he vaulted back afork the saddle as the stallion rebounded. Winded and exhausted by its efforts, the horse could make only a token resistance and even that was soon finished.

Having been acclaimed the winner of the event, Dusty received his prize and congratulations from the Governor. Then he returned Mulcachy's saddle to the barn and made arrangements to have his own rig repaired. He also received Grillman's and Mulcachy's negative reports. Not only had the marshal failed to learn anything from Mark or the betting, but he had been equally unsuccessful at the

2. Produced by breeding a sorrel horse to a dun.

hotel. None of the staff had seen anybody loitering about the building. Nor had any visitor expressed interest in Dusty staying there, or tried to learn which room he was occupying. That information, however, would not have been hard to discover as the register was open on the desk and there had been times when it was not manned. Nor would obtaining access to Dusty's quarters have been too difficult, as each lock was fitted to operate with a master key. A skilled person could deal with such a device easily enough.[3]

Going back to the hotel, Dusty found that the thread was intact when he examined the door. After taking a hot bath and changing his clothes, he went to dinner with Mulcachy. The evening passed enjoyably, with Dusty continuing his work of trying to persuade ranchers that Goodnight's scheme was practical and feasible.

Toward midnight, the small Texan was walking alone on his way back to the hotel. Suddenly he became conscious of being followed. To make sure, he halted and pretended to be looking into the window of a store. Instead, he gazed back along the street. A pair of men had also stopped, but they remained in the shadows and he could not make out who or what they might be.

Walking on, Dusty went faster. So did the men. So he slowed down, waiting for them to come nearer and allow him to learn more about them. Instead of complying, the pair made no attempt to close the distance which separated them from him. Deciding to let them make the next move, Dusty kept walking. Soon the hotel was in sight, and if they had any hostile intentions they would have to take action before he reached it.

"Across the street!" yelled one of the men. "Down!"

Alert for any hint of danger, Dusty reacted instantly. He glanced across the street, seeing a dark shape in the black mouth of an alley. However, fortunately for him, he was

---

3. Belle Boyd proved this in: *To Arms! To Arms in Dixie!*

already diving forward and into the shadows of the nearest building. There was a brief glow of flame from the other side of the street, and as the sound of a revolver's shot reached his ears, a bullet cut the air just above his head. If he had moved a fraction slower, it would have hit him.

Even as Dusty landed on the sidewalk, with a Colt in each hand, and started to twist so that he was facing the shooter, he heard the sound of running feet along the street. A moment later, the man who had tried to kill him was sprinting through the alley.

Despite the warnings he had received, Dusty did not rise from his place in the shadows. He wanted to be sure of the pair before showing himself. While they had saved his life, he still did not know who they might be and their behavior had been suspicious.

Separating, each holding a revolver, one of the men headed for the alley and the other made for Dusty. As he drew nearer, the small Texan saw that he had a badge of some kind on his vest.

"You all right, Cap'n Fog?" the man called anxiously and Dusty identified him as one of Grillman's deputy marshals.

"He missed me," Dusty replied, rising and crossing the sidewalk. "Let's go after him."

Running along the alley, they heard the sound of a horse moving off. There was a shout from the second deputy, followed by a shot, but the hooves grew fainter and there was nothing to suggest that the rider had been hit.

"He got away, blast it!" the second deputy cursed, as Dusty and his companion joined him. "Sorry about that, Cap'n Fog, but we didn't see him until it was too late to stop him shooting."

"I hadn't seen him at all," Dusty confessed. "Not that I'm ungrateful that you were, but how come you've been following me?"

"The marshal told us to, only not to let you know," the

first deputy explained. "He allowed somebody might try to make wolf-bait of you."

"Good of him," Dusty grunted, remembering a comment the marshal had made. "Tell him I wish folks would *start* to ignore me."

14
COLONEL GOODNIGHT'S BEEN KILLED

"We want you to cut out a red and white Box L cow, Captain Fog," Horatio Fitt ordered, indicating a herd of about a hundred and fifty head of cattle which were being held together by half a dozen cowhands. "Start on the whistle."

Two days had passed since the attempt upon the small Texan's life. Although Marshal Grillman had tried, he could not find out who had broken into Dusty's room and damaged the saddle, or discover the identity of the would-be killer. Nor had Mark Counter been more successful, despite his association with Marlene Viridian having developed into an active flirtation. De Froissart and Dolman had not told her of the orders given to Roxterby. In view of his failure to carry them out, they had had no intention of leaving themselves open to her derision by doing so.

To keep up appearances, Grillman had questioned Mark about his whereabouts at the time of the shooting. This had been done in the Belle Grande Hotel, in the presence of Marlene and de Froissart. The woman had given the blond giant an unshakable alibi, by stating that they had been guests at a ball when the attempt was being made.

Realizing that a further visit by them to the Snapping Turtle was almost certain to result in bloodshed and would be unlikely to produce any worthwhile results, Dusty and

Grillman had decided against going there. Instead, as a matter of form, the marshal had requested that Dolman made use of the State Police's jurisdictional powers and carry out the inquiries. Not unexpectedly, Dolman had returned to announce that there was no evidence against Turtle. However, a rumor had started to circulate in Fort Worth that the saloonkeeper was implicated in the attempted murder.

Despite the narrow escape, Dusty had continued with his efforts at gaining further approbation. On the day after the shooting, he had won a contest which had demanded a display of skill in fancy and practical roping. That evening, he had scored another minor victory in the campaign against the hide and tallow men.

Forewarned by Mark, Dusty had countered Marlene's suggestion, regarding Goodnight having ulterior motives for trying to send other ranchers to Kansas, before it could be made and take hold. He had done so by raising the matter himself. Then he had pointed out that although intending to make a drive to Kansas, the colonel had a lucrative contract to deliver cattle to the Army. So Goodnight had no need to worry about selling his stock to hide and tallow factories, especially at the low prices such establishments offered. Listening to Dusty's words and observing their results, Marlene had been seething furiously inside. She could see that there was little chance of the implication stirring up favorable feelings against Goodnight. All it had done was to remind the ranchers of just how little money was to be made by dealing with the hide and tallow men. Not only that, she had sensed a growing belief that driving to Kansas might be a practical proposition.

There had remained only one major doubt. That was how the cattle could be loaded on the trains at the railroad, ready to be shipped to the East. It was, unfortunately, still a subject upon which Dusty could shed little light.

Shortly after noon the second day, Dusty had been told to take his turn in yet another of the County Fair's entertainments. What was more, it was an event in which he had intended to participate even before there had been a need for him to bring himself into prominence as a tophand. There were few things he enjoyed doing more than working with a good cutting horse. To him—and to many other horsemen, even to this day—that was the ultimate form of the equestrian arts. So he had been looking forward with pleasurable anticipation to matching his mount against other first-class cutting horses.

Waiting for the whistle so that he could commence, Dusty sat relaxed on his own saddle. Its maker, Joe Gaylin of El Paso—which was only a small village at that time—was in Fort Worth. He had replaced the ruined rings and the rig was as good as new.

The horse between Dusty's legs was a sleepy-looking *grullo* gelding which he had trained himself. Not more than fourteen hands in height, it lacked the size and presence of the paint stallion. Yet, to the more knowledgeable of the spectators, the *grullo*—its coat slate-colored like a sandhill crane—had the undefinable quality known as *brio escondido,* hidden vigor. It stood as if almost asleep, but with its ears cocked. Alert and eager to move, it never took its eyes from the cattle.

When the judge's whistle shrilled, Dusty did not need to signal for the *grullo* to advance. There was none of the speed with which the paint had taken after the fleeing *golondrino* steer. Instead, the gelding glided slowly and quietly toward the herd.

From his point of vantage on the saddle, Dusty studied the animals. There were bulls, steers, and cows mingled together. From the variety of the brands they bore, they belonged to different ranchers. Dusty was entering into the kind of a situation which frequently confronted a cowhand during a roundup. Not only did he have to locate a specific animal, but he must separate it from its companions. Nor would his task be made any easier by the animal in question being a female.

Looking round, Dusty realized that the cutting out was anything but a sinecure. There were several red and white animals in the herd. He must select the particular specimen nominated by Fitt and without wasting too much time.

While realizing that the test was difficult, Dusty did not feel that he was being victimized. Having won so many previous events, he could hardly expect to have things easy. Nor would he have wanted them that way.

Having seen Lonegron in the crowd, de Froissart left Marlene and Mark. Joining the man, he stood as if watching the small Texan.

"I see Fog's still around," the Creole remarked in a low voice. "You said he wouldn't be after the bucking horse event."

"I'm damned if I know what went wrong," Lonegron admitted angrily, thinking of the chances he had taken to reach the small Texan's room at the hotel, open the door with a simple lock pick, and saw through the saddle's rings. "He must have found out what I'd done. But I was sure he hadn't when I spoke to you at the corral. It looked like the same saddle I'd seen in his room."

"He must have had it repaired," de Froissart commented in a disbelieving tone.

"There wouldn't've been time," Lonegron answered. "Anyways, your man didn't do any better."

"*My* man?" the Creole repeated, sounding puzzled. "But I thought it was *you* who tried—"

"Not me!" Lonegron insisted.

"Then who was it?" de Froissart demanded and seemed so sincere the other man was convinced that he was genuinely mystified.

"I don't know," Lonegron replied. "But, thinking it was you, I started a rumor that it might have been Ram Turtle's doing."

"That's good of you," de Froissart praised.

"Good nothing," Lonegron sniffed. "Now you owe me a favor. I'll be around when I need to collect on it."

"You'll get it," the Creole promised, then grinned. "Turtle's not going to like it."

"Nope," Lonegron agreed, also grinning. "Could be he'll be so riled that he'll take Fog out of the game for us."

"How about Goodnight?" de Froissart wanted to know. "Have you heard from your men?"

"I don't expect to," Lonegron answered. "When they've done their work, they'll head straight back to Quintana. Schelling'll tell me if Fog hears any more."

"I'd be happier if I knew he wouldn't be arriving," de Froissart stated.

"He won't be," Lonegron declared. "I told the boys that if it looked like he'd make it on time, they was to kill him."

While the conversation had been going on, oblivious of everything except the work at hand, Dusty had located the cow. He had identified it, after discarding a red and white bull which bore the same mark of ownership, by its udder and the L brand that had been burned indelibly into its left flank.

"Cut her out!" Dusty commanded, pointing the gelding at the required animal and letting the reins hang loose.

Having been shown what its master wanted, the *grullo* moved closer. Without any fuss, using its weight and an occasional quick nip with its teeth, it started to edge the cow toward the fringes of the herd. It worked with the minimum of guidance from its rider, knowing what was expected of it.

Wishing to emphasize the ability of the *grullo* in carrying out the exacting work, Dusty rested his hands on the horn and allowed the reins to swing freely. He sat well back on the saddle, instead of standing forward in the stirrups as he had when roping the *golondrino*. Cutting involved a lot of rapid changes of direction and the backward seat distributed his weight so as to lighten his mount's forehand as much as possible when making fast turns or whirls.

Watched by the judges, two of whom were working ranch owners who understood what was required in such a task, Dusty and the *grullo* gave a masterly demonstration of cutting out a longhorn. While doing so, the small Texan provided the final and most convincing proof to the doubters among the spectators that he was a cowhand of the first water and could not be dismissed as just another good cavalry officer.

Try as it might, the cow could not rejoin its companions. Every attempt was countered by the little gelding. While the *grullo* used its teeth when necessary, it never did so in such a manner that it chased the cow back to the herd. Always it stopped and turned head to head with her, so as to be able to cover her farther forward or shorter as the occasion demanded. Going slightly ahead in order to halt and swing her, it never looked as if it might commit the blunder of advancing so far that she could duck by and obtain more play in the struggle to return to the rest of the longhorns.

The judges did not only watch for faults by the horse. They deducted points for each step it took when going by the cow, but more could be lost if the rider spurred the outer shoulder of his mount. Nor must he carry the reins level with his upper body, or use them, or his weight, excessively to cue the horse. Picking up and setting the horse was also penalized.

Carefully Dusty and the *grullo* directed the cow away from the herd and toward the cut. At last, she noticed the second bunch of animals and darted in their direction. Satisfied that she did not intend to return to the herd, having seen the same thing happen to another competitor, Dusty brought the *grullo* to a halt. Dropping from the saddle, he praised the little horse while awaiting the judges' verdict. When it was announced, he knew that—with the time he had taken and the points he had been awarded—he stood a good chance of winning. No contestant so far had equaled his score.

"An excellent ride, Captain Fog," Governor Davis praised, having joined in the applause, as Dusty led the *grullo* by his carriage.

"Thank you, sir," the small Texan replied, removing his hat out of deference to the Governor's wife.

"I don't suppose that you've heard when Colonel Goodnight will be arriving?" Davis went on, feeling some other comment was required.

"No, sir," Dusty answered. "But I'll likely be hearing something before too long."

Almost as if wishing to prove that the small Texan was a pretty fair prophet, Schelling chose that moment to come galloping up. His arrival attracted considerable attention, for he was traveling much faster than the pace he usually adopted when delivering a message. Every eye followed him and there was considerable speculation as to whom he would be bearing news. Drawing his mount to a halt, he dismounted and hurried toward the Governor's carriage. However, it was to Dusty that he offered the message which he had taken from his jacket's inside pocket.

"Here, Captain Fog!" Schelling gasped, breathing heavily from the exertion of riding at a gallop from the telegraph office to beyond the city limits where the contest was being held. "I'm afraid it's very bad news!"

"Gracias!" Dusty said, ripping open the envelope to take out and read the message. He stiffened as the words seemed to leap to his eyes, crumpling the envelope involuntarily.

"What is it, Captain Fog?" the Governor inquired and carried on conventionally. "Not bad news, I hope."

Which, in view of Schelling's statement and general air of agitation, might have struck most people as a stupidly pointless remark. However, the news which Dusty had received did not allow him to think about that aspect of the matter. Instead, he handed the sheet of buff-colored paper to Davis.

"My God!" the Governor uttered, staring at the neatly printed message. "Colonel Goodnight's been killed!"

Surprise caused Davis to speak louder than he had intended and the words carried beyond his own party. Listening to the news being relayed through the crowd, passed on by those who had heard the Governor, Schelling scowled. He had hoped to be able to sell the information, as he had the contents of Goodnight's previous message, to Lonegron. There would now be no chance of his doing so. However, he had already received payment for delivering it to Ram Turtle.

Looking around, Dusty saw Mark Counter standing by Marlene Viridian. The big blond met his *amigo's* gaze and made as if to leave the woman. Seeing Dusty give a quick shake of the head, the blond giant remained where he was. It was obvious to Mark that no matter how Dusty felt about the news, he did not want to spoil the friendship that had been built up with Marlene.

"I can't start to tell you how sorry I am, Captain Fog!" Davis said, bringing the small Texan's attention to him. "This is a tragedy and a great loss to the whole State of Texas."

"Yes, sir," Dusty agreed and it was obvious that he had to struggle to prevent himself from showing his true emotions.

"We must cancel the rest of the contest," Davis suggested, nodding to where the judges were hurrying toward the carriage.

"There's no call for that, sir," Dusty objected. "And, happen he could say so, Uncle Charlie wouldn't want to have it done."

"Very well," Davis said, hesitantly and hoping that he was making the right decision. "If you're sure it will be all right—"

"It will be, sir," Dusty confirmed.

Having arrived in time to hear the last part of the conversation, the officials asked Dusty if they could announce the continuation of the contest. On receiving his consent, the owner of the Post Oaks Saloon told the crowd of the decision. He also called for a minute's silence as a tribute to Goodnight's memory.

"How about you, Captain Fog?" Davis asked, looking at the small Texan as they donned their hats at the end of the minute.

"I'd best go into town and telegraph the news to home," Dusty replied. "Uncle Devil has to be told."

"Of course he must," the Governor affirmed. "And while you're at it, I'd be obliged if you'd send word in my name to the State Police in Sulphur Springs. Tell them not to spare any effort or expense to get the men who killed Colonel Goodnight."

"I'll do that, sir, and thank you," Dusty replied. "Now, if you'll excuse me, I'll go and 'tend to it."

"Certainly," Davis replied. "The telegraphist is already on his way back. If you hurry, you'll catch up with him."

"Yes, sir," Dusty drawled and nodded to Mrs. Davis. "Your servant, ma'am."

"The news has hit him badly," Davis informed his wife, watching Dusty riding away. "But he's bearing up pretty well."

Other eyes were watching as Dusty drew rein and spoke a few words to Marshal Grillman, then set the *grullo* into motion. Not the least interested of the onlookers were de Froissart and Lonegron. They had been on the point of separating when Schelling had arrived, but had stayed together out of mutual curiosity.

"Your men have done it!" the Creole declared as Dusty started to ride toward Fort Worth.

"Yeah," Lonegron agreed. "Which means that *we've* got something to do here."

"What's that?" de Froissart asked, although he could have guessed at the answer even before he received it.

"Make sure that Fog's not at the Convention," Lonegron replied. "Because if he wins this event, which looks real likely, they'll listen to him like he was Good-night."

"So we'll have to kill him," de Froissart stated. "The thing is, when and how do we do it?"

"Have him bushwhacked," the other man suggested.

"Not at night," de Froissart protested. "Roxterby said that there were two deputies—"

"So it *was* your man last night!" Lonegron growled.

"Yes," the Creole admitted.

"Don't you trust me?" Lonegron challenged.

"It's not that. Nobody likes to admit they've failed. Any-way, Roxterby's lost his nerve and is already on his way back to Pilar. We can't use him."

"There's plenty more men we can hire, either in town or at Ram Turtle's."

"I know," de Froissart admitted. "But I'd as soon not go there to hire them."

"Leave it to me," Lonegron sniffed. "Only it's likely to cost money and I'll expect you to help me pay it."

"I will," de Froissart promised. "We'll go halves."

Making no attempt to catch up with Schelling and not realizing that plans were being discussed regarding his fu-ture well-being, Dusty rode slowly into the town. Nor did he appear to be in any great rush to dispatch the news and Davis's orders. That was understandable, however, for to any cowhand worth his salt, the welfare of his horse came first.

Walking and leading the *grullo* for the last quarter of a mile, Dusty allowed it to cool down before he reached the livery barn. He removed the bit and let the horse drink from the water trough. There was no sign of human life as he entered the big main building, which did not come as a surprise. All of Mulcachy's staff were attending the cutting horse contest.

Taking the *grullo* into a stall next to the paint stallion, Dusty unfastened the girths and stripped off the saddle. Hanging it on the dividing wall, he started to rub the horse down. Two men entered, looking around. Both were tall, tanned, but dressed in town suits and flat-heeled boots.

"Anybody around, young feller?" the taller of the pair inquired, approaching the stall.

"Not who works here," Dusty replied.

"Can we hire a couple of hosses?" asked the second newcomer, also speaking with a Southern drawl and keeping pace with his companion.

"Like I said," Dusty answered. "There's none of the staff here. But I can show you two that might do."

"I'd be right obliged if you would," the taller man stated. "There's no hurry about it. Finish what you're doing."

"I'll come as soon as I've put his nose bag on," Dusty offered and turned to reach for that item from where it was hanging on a hook at the back of the stall.

"Leave it be," the taller man ordered, whisking a Starr Navy revolver with its barrel cut down to about two inches in length from beneath his jacket. His companion produced a similar weapon and lined it in Dusty's direction. "And keep your hands up there when you turn toward us."

15

THERE WASN'T ANY
OTHER WAY

Just so long as one did not make a single mistake, the easiest person upon whom to compel obedience with a gun has always been a firearms expert. Such a man knew better than to take chances.

Although Dusty Fog would not attain his full potential until the Colt Patent Firearms Manufacturing Company started to market their legendary Model P in 1873,[1] he was already a skilled gunfighter. Even using the long, comparatively cumbersome Colt 1860 Army revolvers, he could rely upon himself to draw with either hand, shoot, and if necessary, kill a man at around thirty feet away in less than a second.

For all that, hearing the man's words, Dusty did nothing more than assess the situation.

Looking over his shoulder, without attempting to lower his hands or turn, the small Texan studied the two men and their weapons. Everything about them warned him that they were probably proficient in using the short-barreled revolvers. The hammers were down in the uncocked position, but he knew that it was not through any oversight on

1. Told in: *The Peacemakers*.

the pair's part. Starr revolvers had a double action mechanism and did not require cocking manually.

"If it's robbery you've got in mind, gents—" Dusty began mildly.

"Do we look like robbers, Chuck?" the shorter man inquired, without allowing his weapon to waver in its alignment.

"I don't know any robbers so's I could tell, Shamp," answered the other, holding his Starr equally steady. "Turn this way, feller, but do it *real* slow."

Covered by the two revolvers, with their owners standing at too great a distance apart for there to be any hope of dealing with them simultaneously—and realizing that nothing else would serve his purpose—Dusty adopted the most sensible course. He did exactly as he was told. Turning around very slowly, he kept watch for the slightest inattention on their part. There was none, so he waited to find out what would be coming next.

"Come out here," Shamp ordered and Dusty left the stall. "Now we'll have your gun belt off. Do it one-handed."

"Whatever you say," Dusty drawled, starting to lower his right hand.

"That's a bad guess," Chuck warned. "We'd sooner have the left 'n'."

While the change of hands would not have been any impediment, for Dusty was completely ambidextrous—having developed that useful trait as a boy, to help divert attention from his small size—he was given no opportunity to take advantage of his captors' ignorance. Using his left hand only, he unfastened the holster's pigging thongs. Then he unbuckled the belt and was told to lay it on the floor and step away from it.

"What now?" Dusty wanted to know, having complied.

"You're coming with us," Chuck answered.

"Where to?" Dusty asked.

"What're you worried about?" Shamp countered, hol-

stering his Starr and picking up the gun belt. "You're coming no matter where it is."

"You're calling the play," Dusty said quietly.

Although the men allowed Dusty to pass between them,
they remained beyond any distance at which he would be
able to tackle one or the other of them. Accepting the
inevitable, he led the way to the front doors. A glance
behind him told him that Chuck was still holding the Starr,
but Shamp had not drawn his weapon.

Leaving the barn, the men moved closer. They were still
separated and just beyond his reach. Yet if anybody had
seen them, they would have looked as if they were all walking along on the best of terms. Not that Dusty expected to
be seen, for the majority of people were attending the cutting horse contest. Even Grillman's deputies, with the exception of one man at the office, were out of town and
policing the crowd.

"Happen we should meet anybody," Shamp remarked.
"You'd best go by like we was all good friends. 'Cause if
you don't, it won't be just you's gets hurt."

"I'll mind it," Dusty assured him.

They did not meet anybody, nor was their journey for
any great distance. Guiding Dusty toward an apparently
empty, small house, Shamp moved ahead. He opened the
door and went inside.

"We've got him, boss," Shamp called, strolling across
what would have been the living room to a door in its rear
wall.

"Don't be bashful," Chuck advised, jabbing his weapon
sharply into the small Texan's back. "Go in."

Advancing across the threshold, Dusty slowed his pace.
He watched Shamp reach the center of the room, but the
"boss" had not yet made an appearance. Dawdling, Dusty
hoped that he would be given the correct response by
Chuck.

He was!

Lulled into a sense of false security by the ease with

which they had captured and brought the small Texan to the house, Chuck became impatient. Wishing to make Dusty hurry, so that he could close the door and prevent any chance passerby from seeing what was going on, the man once more pushed his Starr into the middle of the other's back. At the same time, Chuck used his left foot to shove the door shut.

Feeling the muzzle of the revolver pressing against his spine and hearing the hinges of the door creaking, Dusty deduced correctly what was happening. He knew that his chance had come.

Instantly, Dusty halted and, by bending his knees, dropped his hips as he pivoted his torso swiftly to the right. Driving around as he turned, his right elbow smashed into Chuck's right forearm to knock the Starr out of alignment and away from his body. If the man had been holding a fully cocked, single action revolver, the attempt would have been highly dangerous, if not doomed to failure. However, the Starr's hammer was not at full cock. So more pressure was required on the trigger than would have been necessary to fire a single action weapon. Enough, certainly, for Dusty to believe he had a chance of succeeding in his efforts.

Using his forearm to prevent Chuck from turning the weapon back at him, Dusty took his weight on his right foot and swung his left leg in a short arc. While doing so, he bent his left arm tight alongside his ribs and folded its hand with the thumb uppermost. Swiveling around and using the pressure exerted by his right elbow to turn his attacker's torso away from him, Dusty caused the impetus of the former to aid the blow he struck. Hurling out, his fist caught the man in the kidney region. Letting out an agonized croak, Chuck dropped the Starr and arched his back in pain. Clutching at the point of impact, he staggered away from his assailant.

From dealing, at least temporarily, with Chuck, Dusty devoted his attention to the second of his captors. Having heard the disturbance, Shamp turned. He let the gun belt slip from his fingers to drag for his holstered revolver.

Seeing how fast Shamp was reacting, Dusty moved with even greater speed. Snatching off his Stetson as he started to bound forward, he flung it ahead of him for the vitally important instant required by Dusty. Already the Starr was out and turning into line. Forward thrust the small Texan's left hand to clamp over the man's gun-filled fist. Working in concert with its mate, Dusty's right hand rose to catch hold from underneath. Maintaining both grips, Dusty raised and ducked underneath the trapped limb. Halting behind his captive, with the arm still elevated, Dusty twisted the Starr free with his right hand. The left changed its position to the wrist, bending it down and behind Shamp's back.

Before Dusty could carry out his intention of smashing the revolver's butt onto Shamp's head, Chuck intervened. Ignoring the weapon which he had dropped, he plunged forward. His right hand grabbed Dusty's wrist as it rose to deliver the blow and he hooked his left arm around to encircle the small Texan's throat from the rear. Drawing his arm tight so as to cut off the small Texan's breath, he also shook the trapped wrist vigorously.

If Dusty had been gripping the Starr by its butt and with his forefinger through the trigger guard, he would have been able to retain his hold despite being half strangled and having his wrist shaken. As it was, he lost his grasp on the frame and the weapon clattered to the floor.

For all that he was at a serious disadvantage, Dusty was far from being helpless. Raising his right boot, he placed its sole against Shamp's rump and, releasing the wrist, thrust hard with the leg. Snapping down his foot as the man was propelled across the room, the small Texan shot it behind him so that his heel caught Chuck on the shin. Although the recipient of the kick grunted in pain, he continued to maintain his holds just as effectively.

There was, Dusty saw, no time to waste. He must get

free in a hurry. Having been halted by running into the wall, Shamp was turning and would resume the attack.

Twice more Dusty stamped back at Chuck's shin before he felt the choking hold relaxing and the grip on his wrist was loosened. Exerting his strength, he managed to snatch his arm free. Then he twisted his torso as far as he could with the arm still across his neck. It proved to be enough to let him ram his left elbow into his attacker's chest. Twice Dusty struck, as Shamp rushed toward him, each blow giving him more room to move. Then he caught Chuck's arm with both hands and, pulling it from his throat, used it as a lever to catapult the man over his shoulder.

Releasing Chuck in mid-flight, Dusty watched him crashing down upon Shamp. As the two men went sprawling to the floor, he prepared to dive for and retrieve his weapons. Then he saw that the door to which Shamp had been walking was open. To make matters worse, a large shape that was all too familiar came looking through it. A Remington Double Derringer looked almost minute in the newcomer's massive right fist, but was none the less deadly or dangerous because of that.

"You couldn't get there fast enough," Ram Turtle warned, then flickered a glance to where the two men were rolling apart and sitting up. "You boys stay there. You did *real* good."

"I'll—!" Shamp began.

"Do what you're told," Turtle interrupted. "I'm satisfied. You got him here, which's something."

"Damn him!" Chuck spluttered, rubbing his chest tenderly. "Let me—"

"I told you I'm satisfied!" Turtle snarled, without taking his attention from Dusty for long enough to offer a chance of escape. "Believe me, you don't know how lucky you've been. Get your guns and go wait with the horses."

Muttering under their breath, the two men rose and obeyed. Puzzled by the latest development, Dusty watched them collect their revolvers and slouch from the room. Then he received another surprise.

"You may as well get your'n," the saloonkeeper remarked and changed hands so that he could return the Derringer to its spring-loaded wrist holster. He nodded at the departing pair and continued, "Harwold Cornwall's letter said they were good. He was right. I don't reckon I've anybody who could have fetched you here alive, or would've been willing to try."

"Harwold Cornwall from New Orleans?" Dusty inquired as he went to pick up his gun belt.

"Do you know him?" Turtle inquired, sounding surprised.

"I've heard tell of him," Dusty admitted.

That was something of an understatement. Dusty had had dealings with Cornwall while helping Belle Boyd ruin a Union plot to flood the Confederate States with counterfeit money.[2] While he did not know it, he would in a few years time assist the New Orleans police to bring an end to Cornwall's career as a leader of the city's organized criminal activities.[3]

"Let's talk business," Turtle suggested, watching Dusty buckle on the belt and fasten the holsters' pigging thongs.

"You went to a hell of a lot of trouble just to do that," the small Texan pointed out, wondering when the weight of the belt and its Colts had last felt so comforting.

"There wasn't any other way I could be sure you'd come to see me, or listen to what I've got to say. Anyways, seeing's how Harwold sent them boys along to ask if I'd hire 'em, I reckoned it'd be a good chance to see if they'd be any use to me."

"I hope I haven't turned you off them."

"Nope. They did well enough."

2. Told in: *The Rebel Spy*.
3. Told in: *The Man From Texas*.

"Maybe you'd best tell me what's on your mind," Dusty drawled.

"Do you reckon I tried to have you killed that night?" Turtle demanded.

"Did you?" Dusty countered.

"You're still alive and've got your guns back."

"I'm not gainsaying it."

"Why would I want you dead?"

"Because of what happened when I came to see you with the marshal."

"I'm not saying's I was took with the notion of you coming after that 'breed, 'specially as Grillman didn't have the right to do it," Turtle admitted. "And I had to try to stop you doing it. But it's bad medicine to kill an honest peace officer and Grillman's all of that."

"I'm not a peace officer," Dusty reminded him. "And I'd put lead into two of your men."

"You saved me having to pay 'em at the end of the month's all that meant."

"Did their *amigos* think the same way?"

"Neither of 'em had any friends who'd feel strongly enough to go after you looking for evens," Turtle replied. "And they sure as hell wasn't worth it to me. I was willing to forgive and forget even before you started making money for me by winning those events."

"Why's that?" Dusty asked.

"I don't mind getting the likes of Horatio Fitt riled up at me for what I do to their kin," the saloonkeeper explained. "But I'm a whole lot too smart and careful on locking horns with the kind of backing you've got. And on top of that, the way things are, I'd sooner have you alive."

"So I can keep on winning events?"

"Nope. I want to see Texas set back on her feet."

"*You?*" Dusty snickered.

"Why not *me?*" Turtle challenged.

"I just don't see you as a patriot," Dusty confessed.

"I'm better than that. I'm a money-hungry opportunist."

"I've heard tell of such, but it still doesn't tell me why."

"If Goodnight's notion works out, and I think it will," Turtle elaborated, "there'll be plenty of money coming in from Kansas."

"That's the idea of going up there," Dusty conceded, beginning to see what the other was driving at.

"There's not much cash-money around these days and profits're low, even with the kind of trade I draw in," Turtle went on. "So I'm all for seeing it happen. And you can help bring it off. Fact being, after what happened to Charlie Goodnight—"

"Schelling came to you first, huh?" Dusty growled.

"Don't think mean about folks and reckon I've got second sight," Turtle requested with a grin. "Anyways, I figured you'd be coming in to send the news to Ole Devil, but that you'd likely 'tend to your hoss first. So I sent the boys to fetch you along."

"Just to tell that it isn't you who's trying to have me killed?"

"And that it wasn't me who had Charlie killed. Like I said, I don't want Ole Devil after my scalp. Or you either, if it comes to that. And after this talk that you've been blaming me—"

"Which I didn't start," Dusty stated.

"Somebody did, which I'm not doubting your word," Turtle pointed out. "Thing being who it was's did it."

"The feller who's trying to have me killed'd have a pretty fair reason," Dusty drawled, hoping for information.

"Do you have any notion who that might be?" Turtle inquired.

"Notions is all, but I wouldn't want to name names without having proof. How about you?"

"Was the 'breed tied in with it?"

"Why sure. Him and his *amigoes* had made their play at the Kid. There was two of 'em got away and likely came back to your place."

"I'll not lie to you," Turtle promised. "So I'll just say nothing. You've heard what they say about me?"

"I've heard a lot of things, not many of 'em good," Dusty drawled, but he knew what the saloonkeeper meant.

According to what Grillman had told Dusty after their visit, Turtle had a reputation for never betraying a confidence. The saloonkeeper frequently had messages, information, or requests for assistance to pass on, but he would never divulge a word except to the person for which it had been intended. In that way, he justified the high prices which he charged for his services.

To try to obtain information would be a waste of time, Dusty realized, so he wondered why Turtle had gone to so much trouble to arrange the meeting. There must have been another reason besides a desire to avoid incurring old Devil Hardin's wrath. That alone hardly rated the risks the saloonkeeper had taken.

"That figures," Dusty agreed.

"Happen he's figuring on hiring at my place, he's going to be disappointed," the saloonkeeper continued. "I've passed the word I'd rather you stay alive."

"*Gracias,*" Dusty drawled.

"I heard you had fuss with that big jasper, Counter or whatever they call him," Turtle remarked.

"It wasn't him."

"He'd bear watching."

"It's being done."

"It was a thought," Turtle said. "Hey, though, how do you rate your chances in the Three Miles Stakes tomorrow?"

"Pretty good," Dusty replied.

"Good enough to be sure of winning?" Turtle wanted to know.

"Don't tell me you want to bet on a sure thing, for shame." Dusty grinned.

"I *never* gamble," Turtle objected. "What I do is let

them's wants to do it against me. That way, I'm sure to wind up the winner in the end."

"That sounds like a right smart system," Dusty said sardonically. "Well, I'd best be going."

"And me," Turtle agreed. "So I'll say *adios*, Cap'n Fog. And I'll be tolerable obliged if you don't come to my place again."

"I'll mind it," Dusty promised. *"Adios."*

Walking toward the livery barn, the small Texan wondered what would be the result of Turtle having expressed a desire to keep him alive and unharmed.

Lonegron could have answered that question and to a certain extent did so—although not in Dusty's hearing—when he visited de Froissart that evening.

"We're going to kill Fog tomorrow," the stocky man announced, after ascertaining that they were alone in the Creole's room.

"You hired the men then?" de Froissart guessed.

"The hell I have!" Lonegron snorted. "When my boys tried, they was told that Ram Turtle's passed the word for nobody to take the chore."

"Why did he do that?" the Creole almost yelped.

"I'm damned if I know and the boys'd more sense than try to ask. So we'll do it ourselves."

"We?"

"Me and the boy'll do the killing, but you'll have to help."

"In what way?" de Froissart wanted to know.

"By staying here, in your room, all tomorrow afternoon," Lonegron replied.

"I'll miss the races!" de Froissart protested.

"You'll miss a damned sight more than that if Fog's not dead afore the Convention," Lonegron warned. "And there's going to be all hell raised if he's killed. So if the law comes around asking questions, I want to be able to say we were here, playing poker, all afternoon."

16
GOODNIGHT!

Slowly and remorselessly, Dusty Fog's big paint stallion had been forging ahead of its opponents in the Three Miles Stakes. Some of the riders were using quirts, or the end of their reins, in an attempt to force extra speed from their mounts, but the small Texan did nothing of the kind. Instead, he relied upon his slightly crouching, forward seat and perfect balance which threw the least possible strain upon the swiftly striding animal.

By the time Dusty had reached the point where the trail entered an area of woodland, he was in the lead. Aided by its master's superb equestrian skill, the magnificent stallion's effortless-seeming gait had given it almost a two-length lead on its nearest rivals. For all that, Dusty did not delude himself that the race was won. Not when there were men competing who were almost his equal in riding ability and nearly as well mounted.

Horse racing in Texas during the mid-1860s was far removed from the highly organized and carefully regulated professional sport into which it had already developed in the East. The course bore little resemblance to smooth, level circuits of closely mown grass. Instead, the events took place across country and traversed a variety of terrain. Nor were the horses which competed restricted to selected, specialized thoroughbreds of known ancestry and bloodlines. Anybody with sufficient money to pay the stake fee could enter a mount and run it carrying whatever kind of saddle was fancied.

Bare-headed, Dusty sat his own rig. Although he had left off his rope and Winchester carbine's saddleboot, he had retained his gun belt. Being aware that his life was in danger, he had accepted the penalty of the weapons' weight so that he would be armed and able to protect himself.

Dusty had told Marshal Grillman of the meeting with Ram Turtle the previous evening and they had believed what he had said. That had not prevented the peace officer from keeping the two deputies following Dusty. Nor had the small Texan's objections swayed Grillman from his purpose.

Nothing of importance had happened that evening, except that, in addition to receiving many condolences over the news of his uncle's death, he had been asked to take Goodnight's place at the Convention. He had known that the invitation would not have been made before he had competed in and won so many of the events, including the cutting horse contest.

Nor had anything noteworthy happened during the morning and afternoon. Mark Counter was still escorting Marlene Viridian. While Dolman had accompanied them to the races, Pierre de Froissart was not completing the party. When the opportunity had arisen, Mark had told Grillman that the Creole had said he was staying at the hotel to play poker with friends. Being suspicious by nature and training, the marshal had sent one of his deputies to verify the story. On his return, the peace officer had reported that de Froissart was in his room. He could be seen from the street, seated at a table in front of the window and playing cards. However, the deputy had not been able to see the other players.

Once Dusty had started to get ready for the race, he had put all other thoughts out of his mind. Against the kind of opposition he was facing, he could not afford to let himself be distracted. Winning, however, was of less importance than his success in the earlier events had been with regard to gaining the confidence of the ranchers. He felt that he had already earned that, but meant to do his best and try to win. He had entered the paint, as he had the *grullo* in the cutting horse event, because he enjoyed riding and competing against other men who were experts in equestrian matters.

From the beginning, Dusty had ridden a carefully calculated race. Like all the other entrants, he had been over the three-miles-long circuit and familiarized himself with its physical features.

Although the race had commenced where it would end, in front of the Governor of Texas's carriage, with him doing the starting, on going north from the edge of Fort Worth the riders would be hidden from view in an area of woodland for part of the circuit. The spectators accepted that and many of them used it as an excuse for further betting. There were officials placed at intervals in the woods, to make sure that there was no interference with the race and to prevent irregularities by the contestants.

Flashing by the first of the officials on the edge of the woodland, Dusty hardly gave him a glance. The small Texan's whole attention was on the trail ahead. There was an exceptionally difficult portion about halfway through. Going down a long slope, which would tend to make the horse increase its speed, the route curved sharply at the bottom, passing some densely growing and prickly blueberry bushes. Only a man in complete control of his mount could make the descent and the turn without a considerable slackening of his pace. What was more, it could best be handled without the distraction of other horses and riders. That was why Dusty had been so determined to be the first man to reach it.

Reaching the top of the slope, Dusty looked down through the trees to where the turn must be made. There

should have been three officials at the bottom, ready to
help any rider who found himself in difficulties. Only one
was in sight, a stocky man wearing town clothes. He was
standing somewhat further up the slope than might have
been expected, and even as Dusty looked at him, he spoke
as if to somebody who was concealed behind the trunk of a
massive old cottonwood tree at the side of the trail. Having
done so, the man walked toward the tree.

Starting to go down the slope, the paint increased its
speed. Automatically Dusty adjusted his seat to spread his
weight in a more advantageous manner. Inclining his body
to the rear, he thrust his feet forward in the stirrups and
applied just a little more pressure with the reins. Sure-
footed, despite its size, the stallion continued to plunge
onward, and yet still remained responsive to the signals of
Dusty's legs and hands.

Suddenly the small Texan became aware that there were
two figures dressed in range clothes standing behind the
cottonwood tree. Beyond them, partially concealed
amongst the bushes, lay a townsman. His hands and legs
were bound and there was a gag in his mouth.

Even as Dusty realized the significance of what he was
seeing, the stocky "official" and one of the men started to
make a pulling motion. Rising from where it had been
fastened around the trunk of a post oak, hanging down to
be concealed in a furrow cut across the trail, a rope
snapped right ahead of the small Texan. It was at a height
just sufficient for his horse to pass underneath, but he
would catch his chest and sweep him out of the saddle.

All too well Dusty understood his deadly peril. The stallion's speed was too great for it to make even a sliding halt
on the slope. Nor could he, apart from throwing himself
from the saddle, avoid being caught by the rope. If he
made the attempt while moving at such a pace, he would
be fortunate to alight without serious injury. What was
more, he would still be at the mercy of the men. Leaving
the "official" and his helper to handle the rope, the re-

maining member of the party was drawing his revolver and moving into the open.

While taking in the details, with the stallion rushing ever closer to the rope, Dusty had seen what might offer him his only chance. It was a slender hope and not one which many people would even have considered.

With Dusty, to think was to act. Leaving the reins in his right fist, his left hand flashed across. Out came the Colt from the right side holster, its hammer clicking back. Thrusting forward the weapon, he tried to line the barrel at the slender—but no less dangerous—rope.

Down swung the hammer as his forefinger squeezed the trigger. The Colt roared—and the bullet missed!

Seeing what their victim was trying to do, the "official" yelled something at the man with the gun. Although Dusty did not catch the words, he could guess what had been said, especially as the man lunged forward and started to raise his weapon.

Cocking the hammer with his left thumb, as the Colt's barrel rose from the impulsion of the recoil's kick, Dusty brought it back into alignment. He could see that his position was doubly desperate. Not only was the paint carrying him toward the rope at an ever-increasing pace, but the man was beginning to point the revolver in his direction.

There was, Dusty realized, no possible way in which he could deal with both the threats to his continued existence.

While he was trying to split the rope, the man would shoot him.

Before he could turn the Colt on his assailant, fire, and bring it around to its previous target, the paint would have carried him on to the rope.

Again Dusty's Colt roared, but without any satisfactory result.

The rope remained intact!

It was now not much more than six feet ahead of the fast-moving stallion!

Ignoring the yells of alarm raised by the other riders who

were commencing to descend the slope, the man took a careful aim at the small Texan.

"Don't shoot unless he hits it!" Lonegron yelled, guessing what Dusty was trying to do and helping his other man to keep the rope taut.

While the hide and tallow man had realized from the beginning that there was no hope of making the incident look like an accident, it was his wish to prevent the real motive from being suspected. If Fog was injured by being swept from his saddle, the implication would be that it had been done merely to ensure that he lost the race. Finding that he had been shot, Grillman—a smart peace officer— might consider that there could have been another reason. He could even guess at the truth. Even with de Froissart to supply an alibi, Lonegron had no wish to face the marshal's questioning.

Although the man heard his employer's order and understood what had motivated it, he still took a careful aim at the small Texan. He had been at the Snapping Turtle when Dusty had paid the brief and hectic visit. Having seen how well the young blond could handle a gun, he felt disinclined to take chances.

Once again, Dusty failed to catch the "official's" words. There was, he concluded—having assessed the situation with his usual rapidity—only one course left open to him. It was a desperate and forlorn hope which would hardly be greatly improved even if he had heard Lonegron's instructions. For Dusty's plan to succeed, he would have to rely upon the man at the edge of the trail missing him and, at that range, it was highly unlikely to happen.

With the decision reached and accepted, Dusty diverted all his attention away from the man and his revolver. Rising in his stirrups, the small Texan leaned forward and extended his Colt at arm's length beyond the stallion's head.

Expecting at any moment to feel the man's lead ripping into him, for he dare not spare even a split second to try and see what the other was doing, Dusty watched his Colt's

barrel converging with the rope. He devoted his whole being to holding the weapon steady. There could be no margin for error. He knew that he would have time for only
one shot and must make certain that it did not miss.

There was only one way to do that.

It was a desperate chance!

But it was the only chance he had!

Carefully Dusty manipulated the long-barreled revolver
into position. Its hammer was back at full cock and free to
fly forward. Already his forefinger was starting to squeeze
the trigger, doing so carefully to prevent a premature dis-
charge. With the muzzle almost touching the rope, he com-
pleted the pressure.

Twenty-eight grains of best du Pont black powder detonated, to thrust the conical bullet through the rifling
grooves.

Helped in its work by the muzzle blast burning the fi-
bers, the bullet sliced into the tightly stretched strands.
Dusty saw the rope separate, becoming two lengths which
flicked into the air. Then, as the paint carried him onward,
he heard yells of anger.

Yet the expected bullet had not come the small Texan's
way.

That was not the man's fault.

Certain that he could not miss, with his sights lined on
the center of Dusty's chest, the man had begun to squeeze
the trigger as soon as the rope parted. Even as he did so,
something struck his right temple. It was, although he
would never know, a rifle bullet. Nor did he hear the flat
bark of the rifle which had sent it from some distance away
among the trees. With the lead erupting from the opposite
side of his head, he was flung sideways. The revolver fell
from his lifeless hand without firing and he measured his
length on the ground.

Wondering why he had not been shot, Dusty began to
turn his head. Already he was beyond the cottonwood and
saw the other two would-be killers. The man in range

clothes was clasping his hands, through the fingers of which blood was trickling, to his forehead and twirling around in an unmistakable manner. It was the action of a person who had been shot in the head. Still grasping the end of the rope, the "official" was staggering backward but apparently unharmed.

Suddenly remembering the nature of the terrain, Dusty returned his gaze to the front. The mass of blueberry bushes, thick enough to be very dangerous if the paint should crash into them, were very near.

Fortunately, Dusty's equestrian instincts had caused him to maintain contact with his mount through the reins and bit. Equally luckily, the big stallion was not running blindly. Seeing the bushes, it had started to swerve away from them. Dusty started to guide it around in a circle, meaning to deal with the "official" even though doing so would cause him to lose the race.

Struggling to retain his balance, Lonegron contrived to turn away from the cottonwood tree. He had heard the rifle shots which had ended the lives of his two men, both having been fired practically simultaneously, and wanted to find out who had intervened.

Two riders were galloping through the trees, displaying considerable skill and control of their mounts as they guided the animals with their knees and body weight, their reins being knotted to the saddle horns to leave both hands free to use the weapons.

At the right, sitting his huge white stallion and levering another bullet into his Winchester, the Ysabel Kid looked as mean as a *Pehnane* Dog Soldier on the war path.

In the shape of his body and riding skill, the second of the newcomers had the attributes of a Comanche; except that no member of the *Nemenuh* ever had a beard. Stockily built in the manner of "The People," he wore the attire of a prosperous rancher. The most prominent item of his clothing, giving Lonegron an unnecessary clue to his identity, was a vest made from the black-rosette speckled hide of a jaguar.

"Goodnight!" Lonegron screamed.

The word came out redolent of all the frustrated rage and fury which was boiling inside the hide and tallow man. Clearly the message received by Dusty Fog had been either a mistake or, more likely, a deliberate fake. That was no ghost who came toward Lonegron, feeding another bullet into a Henry rifle by means of the leading lever.

Goodnight was alive!

Snarling curses, Lonegron forgot all idea of escaping. Or he may have realized that he could not hope to do so. Whatever his reason, he had only one thought in his head, to kill the man who had fooled him. Snatching out his revolver, he proved to be both fast and accurate, or lucky. Not quite lucky enough, however. While his bullet tore the hat from Goodnight's head, it did no greater damage. Nor was he granted the opportunity to try and improve his effort.

Still riding at a gallop, the approaching Texans lined their rifles. They fired so close together that the two detonations merged into a single sound. Converging in their flight, the bullets entered Lonegron's chest less than an inch apart, hurling him bodily against the trunk of the cottonwood. For a moment he hung there, the revolver sliding unheeded from his fingers, then he fell onto the rope which ought to have ended Dusty's life.

The small Texan had seen what was happening as he brought his horse around in as tight a half circle as the trees and its speed would permit. Nor did he overlook the other men in the race as they went by. At that moment, he was not interested in them. He was far more concerned with what was going on across the trail.

Recognizing his rescuers, Dusty showed no surprise at one of them being Colonel Charles Goodnight. As soon as he had read the name of the town in which his uncle's death had been reported to have happened, Dusty had known it could not be true. The first message he had received was sent from Sulphur Springs, which had meant that Goodnight would have been well on his way to Dallas by the time the second was dispatched. Guessing what was expected of him, Dusty had gone along with the deception.

"Get going, Dustine!" Goodnight bellowed, reloading his Henry. "We'll see to things here."

"Go win that race, blast you!" the Kid supplemented, sending an empty cartridge case flipping through the ejection slot on top of the Winchester's brass frame. "Why the hell do you reckon we bust a gut coming to save you?"

Acknowledging the words with a wave of his gun-filled left hand, Dusty allowed the big paint to complete the circle and return to the trail as another of the riders tore by. He felt the stallion's eagerness to go after the departing horse and returned the Colt to its holster.

"Yeeah!" Dusty yelled and allowed his mount to have its head.

With the lead the closest of his rivals had built up, Dusty doubted if he had any hope of winning. For all that, he had no intention of giving up. Nor had the stallion. By nature, it was a front-runner and hated to see another of its kind ahead. So it strode out faster and faster, its powerful hind quarters driving it onward with tremendous force and forelegs reaching ahead as if trying to drag the ground under it. Urging it on, Dusty used every trick and skill he possessed to help it run.

Gradually, the paint began to recover some of the ground it had lost while making the turn. It went by one man just as they reached the edge of the woodland and tore on in pursuit of the rest. They were covering the last three quarters of a mile and already going by the first of the spectators.

Crouching forward to cut down the resistance his body offered to the wind, Dusty could feel the mighty propellant power of the paint between his legs. White, foamlike lather flecked its neck and fell from its body, testifying to the effort it was exerting. Dusty was half blinded by sweat, but he did not dare try to wipe it away in case he disturbed his balance and threw his mount off its stride. Soon it had caught up with, and ran between, the two leaders.

First one, then the other of the horses drew just a little ahead of the paint only to fall back into line. Then, with less than a hundred yards to go, Dusty called on his mount for a final effort. Responding gallantly, it started to go even faster. Stride after stride it took, the sequence of its galloping gait continuing in a smoothly flowing rhythm.

Inch by inch, the stallion's head extended before those of its rivals. Their riders were doing everything possible to gain more speed, but to no avail. By that much and no more of a lead, Dusty's mount crossed the line to win the race.

17
YOU MIGHT NOT GET OUT ALIVE

"Well, Dustine, boys," Colonel Charles Goodnight said as he sat with his nephew, Mark Counter and the Ysabel Kid in the dining room of Doctor Sandwich's house. "We got some of them, even if we didn't get them all."

It was Friday evening. The Ranch Owners' Convention had taken place that afternoon. Goodnight and Ole Devil's floating outfit were taking an opportunity to get together so that they could discuss what had occurred, before attending a final reception at the Stockmen's Hotel. They had selected the doctor's home as offering the best chance to prevent Mark's connection with Dusty from being exposed.

When liberated by Goodnight and the Kid, the three race officials had explained that they had been captured by Lonegron's men. None of them had seen the hide and tallow man, as he had kept out of sight until they had been bound, gagged, and hidden among the bushes. However, one had contrived to work his way into the open and it was he whom Dusty had noticed.

On joining the crowd at the finish line, Goodnight had apologized to the Governor for the ruse he had used and had explained his reasons. Wanting help, in view of the various delays which had occurred during the journey, he had sent the first message to Dusty and had relied upon its correct context being understood. By sending the Ysabel Kid, the small Texan had justified his uncle's confidence in his intelligence and deductive ability. What was more, the precaution had proved to be a wise one.

The Kid had arrived in time to prevent Goodnight and the Eastern cattle-buyers from being ambushed a few miles east of Dallas. None of the attackers who had been taken alive could give any information. The two men responsible for the attempt had both been killed and had not told the rest anything except what was required of them.

Although Goodnight had realized that he might be placing Dusty's life in danger, he had arranged—with the help of a friend in Dallas—to send the false report of his death. Again he had gambled successfully on Dusty realizing the truth and acting in an appropriate manner. That had happened, as had Goodnight's hope that the man behind the "accidental" delays and attempted ambush would be brought into the open.

Having arranged an armed escort for the cattle buyers, Goodnight and the Kid had pushed on at a better speed. Reaching the town shortly before the Three Miles Stakes was due to commence, they had learned from Grillman's deputy that Dusty would be riding in it. Remembering what he had seen when examining the course with Dusty, having intended to enter himself, the Kid had realized its potential as a source of danger. So he and Goodnight had set off for the most likely spot, reaching it just in time to play a vitally important part.

Even though the evidence had pointed to Lonegron having been responsible for the attempts to kill Dusty and Goodnight, they had not discounted the possibility of the Pilar Hide & Tallow Company's involvement. Unfortunately, there had been no way in which their theory could be verified.

On being questioned by Grillman regarding his absence from the race meeting, under the guise of the marshal

wishing to disprove certain rumors of his association with
Lonegron, de Froissart had stated that his story of the
poker game was a lie. Having shown almost convincing
reluctance, by pretending to be unwilling to bring a lady's
name into disrepute, the Creole had claimed his real reason had been to hold a clandestine meeting with Marlene
Viridian. However, at the last minute she had sent word
that she had changed her mind and would be accompanying Mark Counter to the races. De Froissart had been angry, but not wishing to make a scene in public, had stayed
in his room.

Admitting that he had known Lonegron and had seen
him on several occasions during the visit to Fort Worth, the
Creole had insisted that they were merely business ac-
quaintances with a mutual interest in discovering the result
of the convention. Repeating that he had had no idea of
what Lonegron was trying to do, de Froissart had declared
that, although his Company might lose money, he wished
to see Goodnight's idea succeed. Realizing that to do otherwise might ruin all hopes of learning the truth about
Dover's death, Grillman had pretended to accept the ex-
planations.

While the Convention had not been an unqualified success, it was sufficiently so to satisfy Goodnight. Not only
had he convinced the majority of the ranchers that it would
be possible to drive their herds to Kansas and show a very
healthy profit, he had provided the solution to the one
question which had baffled Dusty; that of how the cattle
could be shipped.

On hearing of Goodnight's intentions and hopes, Joe
McCoy—a prominent and wealthy Abilene businessman—
had grown enthusiastic about their possibilities. Such had
been his confidence that Goodnight would succeed that he
was having cattle pens, loading chutes, and other amenities
built. Once the herds had arrived, loading the cattle onto
the trains would be comparatively simple.

With that point settled to almost everyone's satisfaction

(there were of course a small proportion who had refused to be convinced) the Eastern cattle buyers had told of their respective companies' interest. While they had not been able to offer contracts, which had been used as proof by the dissenters that they did not believe the herds could be delivered, the buyers had affirmed their willingness to do business in Abilene.

"We never thought we'd get them all," Dusty pointed out. "And, once they see it can be done, the fellers who spoke out against it'll likely start to change their minds."

"Some of them might not have that chance," Mark warned.

"How come?" Goodnight asked.

"Marlene's figuring on asking them to come down to Pilar in a week's time," the big blond explained. "And when they get there, she reckons on persuading them to sign contracts to deliver cattle regularly to the factory."

"You too?"

"Me too, Colonel. Or the R Over C. Only she allows that I should drift down there with her and de Froissart in the morning."

"What did you say to that?" Dusty inquired.

"I told her I'd admire to go along," Mark replied. "When I get there, I'll see if I can find proof that Viridian killed Dover."

"It won't be easy," Dusty stated. "And you'll have to play your cards real close to the vest. Let them find out that you ride for the OD Connected and not the R Over C and you might not get out alive."

"I'll go real careful," Mark promised. "Count on it."

"Did she say why she wanted you to go tomorrow, instead of coming in with the others?" Goodnight wanted to know.

"Not in so many words," the blond giant admitted. "But I get the notion that she might have more than just a cattle contract in mind where I'm concerned."

"Such as?" Dusty asked.

"She's started telling me what a lousy son of a bitch her husband is and how he mistreats her. Could be she reckons I'd make a better one."

"She'd have to be a widow-woman afore she could do anything about that," the Kid pointed out.

"I reckon she could have notions about *that* too," Mark admitted, then glanced at the clock on the wall. "Well I'd best go and get changed, I'd hate to keep the lady waiting."

"How's your shoulder?" Goodnight asked.

"Near on better." The big blond grinned. "Fact being, I'll be able to leave off the sling comes morning."

"That's good," the colonel declared soberly. "Because, one way and another, you could be needing your gun hand afore you get through at Pilar."

Which, as things turned out, proved that Charles Goodnight was more than just a shrewd and farseeing cattleman. He was a pretty fair prophet too.

In her room at the Belle Grande Hotel, while dressing for her rendezvous, Marlene was thinking about what lay ahead. Maybe Goodnight had convinced many of the ranchers that the Kansas business was practicable, but there had been others who had not believed it or would lack the will to try. Sufficient, at any rate, would decline to make the attempt for the hide and tallow factories to continue their operations, if only on a reduced scale. Certainly the profits would be much lower. There would not be enough to share between *five* partners. If she played her cards right, Mark Counter ought to be able to help her solve that particular problem. He would also be of use for another scheme which she had in mind.

While Marlene was planning her future, Gus Roxterby was carrying out the orders he had received from her husband that night outside the hotel. Instead of returning to Pilar, he had visited a ranch at which he had known he would find the kind of men he required. Having done so, he was arranging for them to kill Marlene and the Creole in what would appear to be the course of a robbery as they were returning home.

Due in part to Dusty Fog's efforts and abilities, Goodnight's dream of setting Texas on the road to economic recovery had been put into motion. Soon the herds of longhorns would be on the move and money would be starting to flow into the Lone Star State. However, the small Texan and the rest of Ole Devil's floating outfit were not yet finished with the machinations of the hide and tallow men.

How Dusty Fog learned the truth about Dover's death and what happened when Mark Counter arrived at Pilar is told in:

THE HIDE AND TALLOW MEN

APPENDIX 1

During the War Between The States, at seventeen years of age, Dustine Edward Marsden Fog had won promotion in the field and was put in command of the Texas Light Cavalry's hard-riding, harder-fighting Company "C".[1] Leading them in the Arkansas Campaign, he had earned the reputation for being an exceptionally capable military raider.[2] In addition to preventing a pair of Union fanatics from starting an Indian uprising that would have decimated most of Texas,[3] he had helped Belle Boyd, the Rebel Spy,[4] on two of her most dangerous missions.[5]

When the War had ended, he had become the foreman of the great OD Connected ranch in Rio Hondo County, Texas. After helping to gather horses for the depleted remuda,[6] he was sent to assist Colonel Charles Goodnight and acted as segundo on the trail drive to Fort Sumner.[7] Already acknowledged as a master cowhand, he would eventually gain acclaim as a trail boss,[8] roundup captain,[9] and town-taming lawman.[10]

Dusty Fog never found his lack of stature an impediment. In addition to being naturally strong, he had taught himself to be completely ambidextrous. Possessing fast reactions, he could draw and fire either or both his Colts with lightning speed and great accuracy. Tommy Okasi, his uncle's—Gen-

eral Ole Devil Hardin's—valet, had taught him the Japanese martial arts of jujitsu and karate. Neither had as yet received much publicity in the Western world. So the knowledge was very useful when he had to fight bare-handed against larger, heavier, and stronger men.

1. Told in: *You're in Command Now, Mr. Fog.*

2. Told in: *The Big Gun: Under the Stars and Bars; The Fastest Gun in Texas;* and *Kill Dusty Fog.*

3. Told in: *The Devil Gun.*

4. Further details of Belle Boyd's career are given in: *The Hooded Riders: The Bad Bunch; To Arms! To Arms in Dixie!; The South Will Rise Again;* and *The Whip and the War Lance.*

5. Told in: *The Colt and the Sabre* and *The Rebel Spy.*

6. Told in: *.44 Caliber Man* and *A Horse called Mogollon.*

7. Told in: *Goodnight's Dream* and *From Hide and Horn.*

8. Told in: *Trail Boss.*

9. Told in: *The Man from Texas.*

10. Told in: *Quiet Town; The Trouble Busters; The Making of a Lawman; The Small Texan;* and *The Town Tamers.*

APPENDIX 2

The only daughter of Chief Long Walker, war leader of the Pehnane—meaning Wasp, Quick-Stinger, or Raiding—Comanches' Dog Soldier Lodge, and his French-Creole pairaivo[1] married an Irish-Kentuckian adventurer called Sam Ysabel, but died giving birth to their first child. Given the name Loncey Dalton Ysabel, the boy grew up among his mother's people. With his father away on the family's business of mustanging and, later, smuggling goods across the Rio Grande for much of the time, the responsibility for his education had fallen—in the Comanche fashion—upon his maternal grandfather.[2]

From Long Walker, the boy had learned all those things a Nemenuh[3] warrior was expected to know: how to capture, handle, and train wild horses, or when raiding—a polite name for the favorite Comanche pastime of horse-stealing—to subjugate domestic mounts to his will; to follow the faintest of tracks and obliterate, or lessen, the signs of his own passing; to locate hidden enemies; to live off the country; to move in silence through the thickest cover, even on the darkest of nights; and to be proficient in the use of weapons. In all those he had proved to be an apt and capable pupil. He had also shown a facility for learning languages. By the time he was eleven, he could speak English, Comanche, and Spanish flu-

ently and make himself understood in four Indian tribal tongues. These latter had come from captives held by the Pehnane.

Like any Comanche boy, he had been allowed to accompany his father as a part of his education. Smuggling did not attract mild-mannered saints, but the hardcases along the border had soon learned that it did not pay to take liberties with "Sam Ysabel's kid." Not for nothing had he been granted the man-name "Cuchilo, the Knife" by the Pehnane, *for he was an expert in using one. While not fast on the draw, he could handle his Colt Second Model Dragoon revolver adequately and he had inherited the rifle-shooting skill of his Kentuckian ancestors. The white men along the Rio Grande shortened his name to "the Ysabel Kid," which the Mexicans translated as "Cabrito." Members of both races admitted that, young though he might be, the Ysabel Kid was no easy man to cross. His upbringing had not been calculated to instill exaggerated ideas about the sanctity of human life and he could protect himself effectively against any act of aggression.*

During the War Between The States, the Kid and his father had first ridden as scouts for the Grey Ghost, Colonel John Singleton Mosby. Soon, however, their specialized talents had been utilized by having them collect and deliver to the Confederate States' authorities, supplies which had been run through the U.S. Navy's blockade into the Mexican port of Matamoros. On two occasions, they had found themselves working with Belle Boyd, the Rebel Spy.[4] She had found their knowledge of the border country invaluable.

Sam Ysabel had been murdered soon after the end of the War. While hunting the killers, the Kid had met Captain Dustine Edward Marsden Fog.[5] Engaged on a mission of great and international importance, Dusty had been grateful for the Kid's assistance. When it had been brought to a successful conclusion, learning that the Kid no longer wished to continue a career of smuggling Dusty had offered him employment on the OD Connected ranch. Not as a cowhand, but to

*be a member of the floating outfit[6] where his talents as a
scout would be of great value.*

*The Kid's acceptance had been beneficial to all concerned.
Dusty had gained a loyal friend, ready to stick by him in any
danger. The ranch had obtained the services of an extremely
capable and efficient man. For his part, the Kid was turned
from a life of petty crime, with the danger of it having developed into more serious lawbreaking, and became a useful
member of the community.*

1. *Pairaivo:* first, or favorite, wife.
2. Told in: *Comanche.*
3. *Nemenuh:* the Comanche's name for their nation,
meaning "The People."
4. Told in: *The Bloody Border* and *Back to the Bloody
Border.*
5. Told in: *The Ysabel Kid.*
6. Floating outfit: a group of cowhands employed on a
large ranch to work on the more distant sections of the
property. Taking food in a chuck wagon, or "greasy sack"
on the back of a mule, they would be away for weeks at a
time. Because of General Hardin's prominence in Texas,
the OD Connected's floating outfit were frequently sent to
help his friends who were in trouble or danger. On such
occasions, the Ysabel's Kid's talents were of the greatest
use.

APPENDIX 3

With his exceptional good looks and magnificent physical development, Mark Counter presented the kind of appearance which many people expected of Dusty Fog. It was a fact which they would take advantage of in the future.[1]

While serving as a lieutenant in General Bushrod Sheldon's cavalry regiment, Mark's merits as an officer had been overshadowed by his tastes in uniforms. Always a dandy, and coming from a wealthy family, he had been able to indulge his whims. His clothing, particularly a skirtless tunic, had been much copied by the young bloods of the Confederate States' Army, despite considerable disapproval on the part of crusty senior officers.

When peace had come, Mark followed Sheldon in Mexico to fight for Emperor Maximilian. There, he had met Dusty Fog and the Ysabel Kid and helped with the former's mission.[2] On returning to Texas, Mark had also been invited to join the OD Connected's floating outfit. Knowing that his brothers were sufficient to help his father, Big Rance Counter, to run the great R Over C ranch in the Big Bend country—and suspecting that working with Dusty would be more exciting—he had accepted.

At the time of the Tarrant County Fair, Mark's name had not become generally connected with Dusty Fog and the OD

Connected. Soon, however, he would be accepted as the small Texan's right bower.[3] He would gain fame for his Herculean strength and prowess in a roughhouse brawl, but—due to being so much in Dusty's presence—his true capability with his Colts would receive little attention. Men who were in a position to know said that Mark ran Dusty a very close second in speed on the draw and accuracy.

1. Told in: *The South Will Rise Again.*
2. Told in *The Ysabel Kid.*
3. Right bower; a term in the game of Euchre, meaning the second-highest trump card.

J.T. EDSON

Brings to Life the Fierce and Often Bloody Struggles of the Untamed West